Traegonia
The Sunbow Prophecy

Written by
K.S. Krueger

Illustrated by
Dino C. Crisanti

Outskirts Press, Inc.
Denver, Colorado

Traegonia
The Sunbow Prophecy
All Rights Reserved.
Copyright © 2011 Traegonia Inc.
v3.0
Written by K. S. Krueger
Illustrated by Dino C. Crisanti

First book, second edition in the Traegonia Series
Ages 8 and up
Fantasy Fiction, middle grade fantasy fiction, all age's fantasy adventure

Outskirts Press, Inc.
http://www.outskirtspress.com

ISBN: 978-1-4327-7603-9

Library of Congress Control Number: 2011911809

Outskirts Press and the "OP" logo are trademarks belonging to Outskirts Press, Inc.

PRINTED IN THE UNITED STATES OF AMERICA

Dedicated to
All Who Believe!

Contents

Prologue

Traegons are a community of beings who live in a place known only to them as Traegonia. You will not find this place on any map, for it is everywhere and it is nowhere. In some regions of Traegonia, their land is covered with huge trees, which provide them everything necessary for their survival. They make their homes deep within the forest in caves, old hollowed-out trees, and beneath the earth. Their homes are simple; furnished with items they make themselves and those that they trade with others within their community. Occasionally, they find strange items within the boundaries of their land, which they enjoy incorporating into their home décor as well as in their personal embellishments. Everything comes from the earth and is honored and held sacred. They live simple lives, with complete respect for the land and all that surrounds them; never hoarding their natural resources and ensuring that the needs of those in their community are met. Their food consists of different types of small game, assorted insects, and that which comes forth from the earth's surface. They work together to ensure that no one goes hungry.

At first appearance, they can seem a bit frightening, but once you have peered into their wise and kind eyes, that speculation quickly dwindles. Standing two feet at their tallest, they have quite a grand presence. Each has their own interesting personality and developed skills, and holds their own place within the community. They live a peaceful co-existence with the earth, all of nature, and each other, free from war and hatred. They are quite intelligent and cunning though, which I suspect is how they have managed to remain hidden and undiscovered.

Uncivilized in appearance only, they are a rare group who have much to teach, living what we might consider, 'the old ways'. How long they have lived is a mystery, but their culture and existence gives much to be explored. Where exactly they dwell, I will never divulge, as I made a promise long ago. Though they have recently informed me that now is the time for me to share my knowledge of them with others, in the hopes that we as people, thought to be truly civilized, might benefit from their teachings. Of course, they know that we exist, they have known for a very long time, as we have not been as discrete. They worry though, about the impact of our actions upon the earth and ultimately upon ourselves. They have now given me permission to tell their story, or at least parts of it. Their kindness and willingness to share their wisdom, even at the risk of being discovered, has given me the strength to try as best as I am able to tell their story. I was quite young when I first discovered them, or maybe I should say when they discovered me…

Chapter 1
Learning of Their Existence

For as long as I can remember, when there was free time from work and chores, my mom and dad would pack a picnic lunch and we would head off to our favorite woods where we could picnic, and dad could spend the day fishing. Mom would lie on a blanket and read a book, or just soak in the sun's warm rays. My dad was content to sit by the water with a few poles cast and wait. The only time he would return from his respite was occasionally for lunch or when it was time to go home at the end of the day. My favorite thing to do was to venture into the woods. Sometimes, I would walk so far into the woods that the branches from the trees would almost completely cover the sky and only streaks of sunlight would stream through the darkness. One time, I was pretending that I was all alone, far away from my home and any other humans.

It was quiet and so was I. I picked up a stick that would serve as my machete, and began clearing the thick brush and hunting for my next meal, which could quite possibly be the only meal I would have for days. I was searching for a lion, a moose, or possibly a wild boar, something big enough to feed me for many a week or maybe more. I heard the sound of rustling leaves and crackling twigs. I stopped suddenly, and carefully listened for which direction the prey was hiding. I crouched down and moved slowly off the path. I began to crawl in the direction of the sound. Each time I moved, the thing, my dinner, would stop. I would pause as well and wait for some more movement to indicate which way I should go. There it was again; in my mind I thought of a large beast, frightened by my scent: the scent of a mighty hunter. The sound was close, coming from just ahead behind a large bush. I could hear my breath and imagined the fear the creature must be feeling. I stood and ran fast toward the bush, machete in hand. As I came close, I heard something coming at me through the leaves from under the bush, it ran straight at me and then turned quickly and disappeared through the trees. I gasped and my eyes widened when I first heard the sound coming at me, but then I had to laugh because, great hunter that I am, I was being charged by a large bunny rabbit.

As I stood there laughing at myself, I felt something hit me in the head. I looked around, but I didn't see anything. *Probably a stick fell from the trees*, I thought. I started to walk back, scouting for good trees to climb after lunch, and then I got hit in the head again. It wasn't hard and it didn't hurt, it was just strange I guess. This time I saw the thing hit the ground, so I walked over and picked it up. It was an acorn. I looked up at the trees for a crazy squirrel, because I know they can be funny like that, but I didn't see anything. I felt a chill run up the back of my neck. I tried to shake off the nervous feeling and continued walking up the path. Again I was hit, this time it bounced off my shoulder. I looked at the trees around me and noticed that not one of them had acorns on it.

"Okay, what's going on? Who's out there?" No one answered and I guess I didn't expect anyone to either. The hair on my arms stood up this time. "It's not funny, you know," I blurted out. I began to walk faster up the path, almost at a slow jog. I looked back a couple of times, but saw nothing. I was also watching the ground in front of me because people always trip and fall when they're being chased in scary movies, and I've always thought it was sort of stupid. *Just watch where you're going and you won't fall.* I thought to myself. I started to pick up speed, my heart was pounding in an excited fear. I could see the opening in the forest where I had come in. I was almost there, and then I did it. I tripped and fell hard. I slid a little kicking up the leaves and sticks that were lying on the path. When I looked back, there was nothing in the path that I could have tripped on. Not a rock or root coming up from the ground, nothing. I scrambled to my feet and sprinted for the exit.

Finally, I was back at the blanket with my mom, covered in dirt and with a stray twig in my hair. She giggled and questioned me about where I had been, and what on earth I had been doing. I told her about my adventures, imagining I was a great hunter, tracking animals and finally, the acorns that spooked me into fleeing from the woods. When I got to the part about my fall, I noticed that she was smiling at me with what looked like a knowing smile.

"What, what do you know?" I exclaimed, in a pleading tone.

"Sit down and listen carefully," my mom stated in a quiet, secretive voice, still with that smile on her face. "In all of the forests, there are many animals who dwell there, birds, squirrels, snakes, rabbits, and many, many others. There is also something else that dwells there too."

The way she said that made the hair on the back of my neck stand up again. Thoughts of horrible, hairy monsters raced through my mind. *How could she let me go out there, knowing that these terrible creatures were lurking?* I gulped, thinking to myself. I had a feeling she could tell what was going through my mind.

She took my hand and looked into my eyes. "Oh, my son, they are not to be feared, they are magical creatures of the forest. They are fairies, gnomes, sprites, and as many different names as you can think of. They do not wish to be discovered, so people rarely ever have the opportunity to see them. They are not dangerous, just mischievous." She paused and smiled again. "Maybe it was one of them who threw the acorns and tripped you."

I lay on the blanket, staring into the sky, watching the clouds as they created a floating picture show across the bright blue background, thinking about what my mom had told me and wondering just what these creatures might look like. That day, I was amazed, my curiosity sparked, and I was sure that the next time I went into the forest it would be very different. I could never view it again the same as I had before.

From that day on, whenever I ventured into the forest, I was quiet and very aware. I moved like a spy trying to catch a glimpse, but most of the time I never saw anything at all. I would hear something rustle through the leaves, but it would only turn out to be a couple of squirrels playing, or a frightened rabbit trying to find his way home.

One day, however, my patience and curiosity paid off. I had gone into the forest, deciding to sit quietly, watching and waiting. I snuggled my body down very close to the ground. Lying on my stomach, I moved some leaves around and over me. Being so still and so quiet for so long, I must have closed my eyes and drifted off to sleep. How long I was asleep, I cannot be sure, but it was the whispers that broke into my sleep, into my dreams that caught my attention.

"Shh, Karia, do not wake him. He will discover us, and then we shall be in great trouble."

"Juna, it appears that his mim is calling him. She will worry so and come looking for him. She will never find him covered in all these leaves."

"Then, Karia, I suppose we should uncover him, but then we must get on to our own work."

During their whispered conversation, I opened my eyes slightly, slowly, so that they wouldn't know I was awake. They were not fairies as I had seen in books, but they were incredible, whatever they were. I thought their skin resembled the bark of a tree, and their knuckles were like the knots. It looked as though it might be softer to the touch than a tree. Their faces were long, kind of like a dragon or something. Their hands and feet were large compared to their bodies, almost like a dinosaur but they walked upright like us. Their clothes looked to be handmade and tied with other pieces of fabric. The one called Juna had long white wavy hair, and his ears were large and pointed, standing taller than his hair. He had a long square jaw with a long curved tooth poking out on one side of his mouth. He looked quite strong for his small size.

The one called Karia had hair that looked like long tan and black feathers, and though her ears were also large, they lay back along the side of her head. It was clear that Karia was a girl, because she wore a type of dress and was much thinner and not as muscular looking as Juna. Her hands were also slightly smaller than his, as was her face, and she didn't have that strange tooth.

Carefully, they moved around me, removing leaves very, very gently, trying hard not to wake me. In the distance, I could hear my mom calling.

"Dino, Dino, it's time for lunch, come out of your hiding place at once." Her voice sounded stern but with a bit of concern.

I wanted to get up and run to her and tell her what I had seen, but I wasn't done seeing yet, and I was a little afraid of what they might do if I woke up and startled them.

"Karia, hurry, she is coming closer," Juna cried with distress in his voice.

"I am moving as fast as I am able, Juna, but I wish to look at him closer, this is the first time I have ever seen a human this close," Karia replied.

"There is certainly no time for discovery, if he awakens he may try to catch us, or worse, tell others like him about us. We are in grave danger just trying to help him." Juna said trying to hurry Karia, looking back toward my mother's voice.

"But, Juna, he seems so innocent, sleeping. Maybe he is the one the Wayseers have spoken of, the one who may understand our kind, the one we will be able to trust," Karia whispered, carefully looking me over.

"This is not for you and I to determine, we are but young ones, and besides, if we are caught even being this close to a human, we would find ourselves a sure punishment waiting when we return home," Juna answered very seriously.

Just then a small gnat flew straight up my nose and I couldn't keep myself from letting out a much-needed sneeze. "AAAHHH Choo!" Leaves blew all around my head. I sat straight up and looked around. I saw no one, they were gone. I looked everywhere hoping to catch one more glimpse of them, but there was nothing.

Did I dream the whole thing? I questioned myself. *How could they just disappear like that?* I was so confused. My mom must have heard my sneeze also, because when I looked up, she was coming toward me down the path.

"I have been calling you, young man, for the last ten minutes. Why didn't you answer me? I was beginning to get scared. If you are going to ignore me, you will not be allowed to have your adventures in the woods anymore," scolded my mom.

"I'm sorry, Mom. I didn't mean to make you worry. I must have fallen asleep and didn't hear you calling," I apologized. "I promise not to fall asleep again while on my adventures."

"Alright then, come on now, it's time for lunch."

As we walked back to our picnic spot, my eyes searched everywhere, on the ground, in the trees, far beyond the path, but there was nothing, no sign of them at all. I remained preoccupied throughout lunch, just trying to figure out if it was real or just my imagination.

Karia's and Juna's hearts were pounding as they slowly opened their eyes. "Karia, do you realize how near we came to being discovered? It is a very good thing that humans do not see or smell quite well," said Juna, sounding scared and upset.

"That was so exciting, don't you think? We were so close to him. Besides, I do not feel that he is dangerous. He did not smell evil. And did you see, he did not even say anything to his mim about us?" responded Karia.

"What do you know about how evil smells, do you think you are a young Wayseer or something? You are merely a young one with a colorful imagination. And how can you be sure that he will not, or has not already told his mim or others for that matter? They could be forming a hunting party as we speak, and planning their kill," replied Juna after taking a breath.

"Now who has the colorful imagination? You are acting like a frightened little bird, now calm yourself. And who knows, I just might become a Wayseer, or even the next Oracle," rebutted Karia. "And you, Juna, will always remain a cowardly commoner."

"Mind your words, Karia, most powerful Oracle young. You had better remember where your roots began, for you also come from a fine family of commoners. Well, I suppose we had better find the rest of the bark that Mim needs for her teas," said Juna. "Or you will have to cast us a great spell to get us out of the trouble we'll be in."

Chapter 2
First Meeting

My mom laid out a very nice lunch that she had prepared, she placed mine in front of me and walked to the riverside with dads. I sat and ate, thinking about all that had just happened. I decided not to tell anyone what I had seen; I figured that no one would believe me anyway. Well maybe my mom would, but I guess I just knew that now wasn't the right time. I ate in silence, daydreaming about seeing them again. Mom returned and ate quietly with me. I hoped she was not still angry about earlier. After we finished eating, and Mom was putting things back into the basket, I asked if I could go back out to continue my adventure. She looked at me and then removed her watch from her wrist and handed it to me. "Be back in exactly one and a half hours, we will be leaving then and I don't want to have to come looking for you again."

I put on her watch and smiled at her. "Thanks, Mom, you won't have to come looking for me again."

I took a handful of my mom's homemade trail mix and headed back to the place where I had fallen asleep earlier. Nearing the spot where I had first seen them, I moved slowly and listened carefully in an attempt to try and locate them. I sat down under a nearby tree, and hoped desperately that they had not left. After waiting a few moments, I heard a rustling in a nearby tree. I looked up and there they were, busy doing something, I wasn't sure what, but it looked important.

―――――――――((()))――――――――

Karia and Juna moved intentionally about the tree, looking very closely at the bark. I moved in closer in order to better see and hear what they were doing. They seemed to make an unspoken agreement that a certain area of bark from the tree was just what they were looking for. Both of them were on the same branch; Karia on one knee and Juna standing behind her. I heard them speak at the same time, slow and serious.

"Tall and strong you stand, full of great wisdom,
giving freely of yourself, that our needs may be met.
As we take of your being we do so with gratitude and thankfulness.
We leave with you in return this poultice, to nourish you
and our prayers, that your healing may be rapid.
With Honor and Respect."

They stood quietly for a moment and then the one called Juna stepped forward. He began cutting away at the bark of the tree, with a crude-looking knife. Chipping a circle in the bark, he pulled it off and placed it, piece by piece into a red cloth bag that the one named Karia held open. Once the circle was completely cut away, she removed a wooden container from a pouch she carried on a sash around her waist. She moved forward, opened the container, and began to spread a liquid of some sort on the spot where the bark had been removed. Then with open hands, together they both touched the tree and stood quietly for another moment.

———— ⊰«◉»⊱ ————

I was crouching behind a nearby tree watching them work when I lost my balance and took a step. I must have stepped on a stick; the cracking sound broke the silence like a train wreck. I looked briefly at the ground and then up again into the tree and in that instant they were gone. I blinked hard in an attempt to focus again, but I didn't see them anywhere. Once again, I began to question myself, and what I'd seen, so much so that I pinched myself to see if it was possible that I had fallen asleep again.

"Ouch," I said aloud. "How can they just disappear like that? No sound, no nothing." I sat down against the tree, and lay my head in my arms, disappointed in myself for having been so clumsy.

———— ⊰«◉»⊱ ————

Once again, Karia and Juna's hearts were pounding. "He could have tried to catch us or scare us or even throw things at us, but he did not," Karia said to Juna.

"We do not even know how long he was there, Karia, and if he was there very long, then we are becoming lax with our senses," breathed Juna.

"Well, I wish to meet him, Juna, I do not sense any danger about him. You may wait here if you so desire, and watch out for me. If anything happens, you can come and save me, okay?" Without waiting for a response from Juna, Karia set off quietly down the tree to meet the boy.

"Dino, is it? Is that your name?" Karia spoke very directly.

I raised my head, startled and just stared straight ahead. "Uh... yes that's my name. Wwwhat is yyyours," I stuttered.

"Karia, is my name. What is it that you want? Why have you been watching us?"

My head was flooded with questions of my own in response to hers. *Who are they? What are they? Where are they from?* So many questions, but I didn't just want to start babbling questions at her, so I just said... "I don't want anything, well, I guess I just wanted to meet you."

"How did you know about us, how did you know we were here? Did someone tell you about us? Did someone send you here?" Karia sounded strong, as if reprimanding me for being here.

"No, not at all, I came here with my mom and dad to picnic and fish. I love the forest, so I take adventures by myself just to see what I can see. Well, today I saw you. I don't want to hurt you; I guess I just wanted to watch you and to meet you. Who are you if you don't mind me asking?"

"Actually, that is a difficult question for me to answer, as we do not usually speak to humans, and really do not wish to be known. Telling you anything could endanger all of our kind. Can you understand that?" stated Karia directly.

"Yes, I think I understand. Are you afraid I will tell others about you and lead them here to you?" I asked.

"Yes," she agreed. "The only reason that I am speaking with you at all is that I sense goodness within you. Am I correct in what I sense?"

"I think that you're right, after I first saw you I just felt that I shouldn't tell anyone about you. Not even my mom, who I am very close to. I guess I knew in my heart that meeting you and knowing that you exist is something I must keep to myself. And I believe that this is something I can promise to do," I replied proudly.

I thought about the trail mix in my pocket and decided to offer some to Karia. The sun reflected off of the watch my mom had given me to wear. A spot of light danced across the ground and the trees as I moved my hand. Karia watched carefully, cocking her head at the watch on my wrist.

"What is that sparkling thing tied to your arm?" she asked curiously.

"Oh, it's a watch. It belongs to my mom. She wanted me to wear it so that I will know when to be back."

Pulling the trail mix out of my pocket, I asked, "Would you like some trail mix? My mom makes it. It's very good."

Karia watched my every move very intently. "What is a watch? How can it tell you when to go home? Does it speak? And what is the sparkling thing that hangs from the side of it?"

I giggled as I tried to answer her questions. "A watch is something that we use to tell time, it's like a really small clock. It doesn't speak, you have to read what it says."

I reached over to touch the small charm that dangled from the band. "And this is a charm; a silver figure of a dolphin. My mother really likes dolphins. Do you know what a dolphin is?"

Karia looked closer at the charm on my mom's watch. "No, I have never seen a dolphin but it looks to be a fish of sorts. The charm is very beautiful, may I have it?" Karia's eyes moved from the watch to my hand, where I still held the trail mix. "What is this?" she asked, even before I could answer her about the charm.

"It's a mix of dried fruit and nuts. It's very good, try some." I held out my hand for her to take some.

Karia reached into a pouch tied around her waist. She pulled out a smaller pouch and opened it. "We too have what you call a trail mix, which our mim also makes. You may have some of mine as well."

Karia took a bit of my trail mix and placed it into her mouth. Then she held out her pouch to me. I looked into the pouch and swallowed hard. It definitely wasn't dried fruit and nuts. I raised my eyes to her. "What exactly is in your mix? I asked.

"Crushed and dried berries, shaved sweet willow bark, dried ticks, and sun-dried ladybugs," she answered almost matter-of-factly. She motioned me to hold out my hand and she poured some out. I looked at it again, and not wanting to make her feel bad, I picked out the ticks and ladybugs and put them back in her bag.

"I am allergic to insects. They make me break out in hives." This wasn't exactly a lie; I probably would have broken out into something if I were to eat those bugs. Yuck!

"That's too bad, they are very tasty," she responded, watching for my response to her mix.

"Mmmm," I hummed, as I chewed the mix after quickly popping it into my mouth, trying to dismiss the thought of some tick leg stragglers making their way to my stomach. Actually, it wasn't that bad; a little dry, but not too bad. "Thank you, your mom must be a good cook," I said politely.

"More?" she asked, holding out the bag again. "Yours was quite good as well."

"No, thank you. I'm kind of full from lunch. Would you like some more of mine?"

"Yes, I would like that very much." She held out her hand.

I had almost forgotten that there were two of them until I glanced up and saw the other one standing off about five feet from where we were sitting. Without even turning around, Karia glanced up at me and said, "Dino, this is my brother, Juna."

I looked at him again and nodded.

"Come over and join us," Karia told Juna, still eating the trail mix. "It is about time you decided to come down out of that tree. I was beginning to think that you too had fallen asleep. Dino is sharing something he calls trail mix, and I have offered him some of Mim's Traegon Mix."

Juna walked over and stood silently. I looked at him intently. In my seemingly normal conversation with Karia, I had almost forgotten how different they looked. He seemed quiet and careful, studying Karia and me. I didn't know what to say to him, I could tell that he was uncomfortable with our meeting. I guess I really couldn't blame him. I'm sure the fear of a stranger and of possibly being found out was immense. Juna looked at me and then at Karia, and finally sat down. Karia broke the awkward silence.

"Have something to eat." She handed her bag of mix to Juna.

"What is your plan, Karia, now that you have met him?" Juna spoke as if I were not even there.

Karia was still admiring the watch and the charm that hung gracefully from its band. "Look at this, Juna, is it not beautiful? It is a dolphin. Is it a large fish or a small fish?" Karia asked, turning the conversation back to me.

"A dolphin isn't actually a fish at all," I responded. "It does live in the water, but it breathes air through a hole in its back. They are very big, as big as me, and even bigger. They live in the ocean."

Karia looked up at me with wide eyes as I described these great creatures. "I do believe I may have heard of these creatures before," she said. "I believe that the Traegons that live near the big waters have spoken of them. They are friendly, are they not?"

"Yes, I've heard that they are." She seemed so fascinated with the story and the charm that I had an overwhelming urge to give it to her. I opened the ring at the top of the charm and slipped it off the band. "Here, Karia, you may have this." I handed the charm to her.

"Your kindness is deeply appreciated," she replied, and respectfully bowed her head. She then reached into her pouch and pulled out a beautiful stone. As she handed it to me, she said, "And this is for you, my friend."

I took the stone and looked at it closely. It was more beautiful than anything I had ever seen. It was long and clear with points at both ends. As I held it to the sunlight, I could see that there was a beautiful rainbow inside, running from point to point.

"Thank you, I have never seen a stone like this before, and the rainbow is so clear," I told her.

Karia looked at me strangely. "It is a crystal. They are very special to our kind. But there is not a rainbow within, for it is not raining. What lies at the very center of this crystal is a sunbow, and to catch a sunbow within a stone such as this is a very magical gift. I have always carried it with me, and now the magic of the sunbow is yours," Karia stated wisely.

"We will need to go soon," Juna broke into the conversation.

I looked at my watch and knew that I too would have to be getting back. "When will I see you again?" I asked.

"We are never far," responded Karia. "The next time you are in this forest, come to this spot and call our names. We will know that it is you and we will come. But until that time, please do not tell anyone of our existence. It could be devastating to our kind."

"I promise, I won't tell anyone," I replied. "Thank you, for everything. Goodbye."

"Until we meet again." Karia smiled.

I watched as they walked back toward the tree I had seen them in. I blinked and they were gone. *I need to ask them how they do that,* I thought to myself. I stood up and walked quietly down the path. No longer did the deep woods frighten me, for now I had two new friends here. This was the greatest adventure of all.

When I got back to the picnic spot, my mom was already packing up. I have always been close to her, and wanted so much to share my experience with her. I know that she would have been just as excited as I was, and that she would not have told a soul if I asked her not to. Still, I made a promise to Karia, and this was one promise I had to keep.

"Back just in time," my mom called, as I walked toward her. "Help me fold this blanket. We'll be leaving soon. Did you have a good adventure?"

"Yes, Mom, I did. I really like these woods. Will we be coming back here again next weekend?" I asked, trying not to sound too anxious.

"I suppose that will depend on how the fishing is," she answered, as she looked off toward the river.

Just then, my dad approached from the hill leading up from the riverside, gear in hand. My dad always loved fishing; I think it relaxed him. He tried to teach me once, but I can't seem to sit quietly enough for long enough. He said I don't have the patience. I think I am learning more about that now. I ran toward him to see if I could help him carry his gear.

"Did you catch anything?" I asked, as I took his tackle box.

"I caught some small ones, sunfish and blue gill mostly. I had one good bite though, maybe a bass. I guess we'll just have to try for him again next weekend," my dad told me, as we continued toward Mom.

My heart raced with excitement, I could hardly keep from jumping up and down. We would be coming back again for sure, I couldn't wait!

Chapter 3
Trouble in Traegonia

On their return trip home, Karia and Juna discussed whether or not to tell their parents about Dino. They walked in silence for a long time before Juna spoke.

"The boy seemed kind," Juna said, beginning the conversation.

"Yes, he was very gracious, wasn't he? I do hope that he returns again. I was very interested in his words and his ways. I wish to know more about his people. I wonder if they are all like him," Karia responded thoughtfully.

"Do you think that we should tell Mim and Sire Argus about the boy?" asked Juna. "Do you think that they will be angered at our revealing ourselves to him?"

"I cannot be sure, Juna, but I have this feeling. There is something special about him. I think that we should also inform Oracle Balstar of his existence. Maybe he will be able to tell us more about him, and what it is that he might want," answered Karia, deep in thought.

Juna put his hand out to stop Karia, took a deep breath and looked her in the eye. "This could get us into a great deal of trouble, you know. Do you understand this?"

"I understand, but do we have any other choice at this point?" Karia questioned, but Juna was silent. "I didn't think so." They continued on their way.

Finally, Juna reluctantly agreed that they would speak to Mim and Sire Argus and ask them to contact Oracle Balstar. They completed their walk home in silence.

Karia and Juna's family had made a modest home within an old walnut tree. This was a good home because the tree had grown to an enormous size, which allowed them plenty of space to dwell comfortably. It also bore a great deal of nuts, which they were able to store for times when the hunting was scarce. Sire Argus had made most of the furniture himself; he was quite a craftsman. Mim was very talented at sewing and weaving, and always ensured that there was plenty of good clothing for all. She was also very knowledgeable about herbs and could treat whatever illnesses might threaten the family.

As Karia and Juna approached their home, they were greeted by Miracle, a young squirrel that lived at the very top of their tree. One spring day, when Karia and Juna were new, there was a terrible storm and a large oak nearby was struck by a bolt of lightning. The squirrels' nest at the top of the tree fell all the way to the ground. It was quite sad, the whole family was killed except for one tiny young squirrel. Mim and Argus said that it was a miracle that he had survived, and the name became his. Karia and Juna grew up with Miracle, thinking of him more as a brother than a pet. He eventually moved to the top of the tree, as squirrels are not generally pack animals, but was always close by, greeting the family whenever they returned home from any journey.

Juna pulled some pine nuts from his pouch and rattled them in his hand as they approached the tree. Moments later, Miracle scurried down the tree and hung by his back legs. Stretching his body and his tiny arms, he sniffed the air and reached out for the nuts that Juna was offering. After filling his cheeks with the nuts, he looked directly at the two of them and sniffed again. Sensing that they had been somewhere they shouldn't have been, he immediately turned, ran up the tree, and then circled back down, all the while chattering in a very nervous manner. Finally, he disappeared into the top of the tree.

Juna looked at Karia, "It seems that he is aware of something. He must smell the boy's scent. Karia, we will be in grave trouble if Mim and Sire Argus smell the boy too."

"Only if it is before we are able to explain ourselves. You must try not to worry so much, Juna," Karia responded.

Once inside, Karia and Juna removed the bark from their pouches and handed it respectfully to Mim.

"Ah, the bark I have been waiting for. Thank you, my younglings, you have done a fine job."

"Where is Sire Argus?" asked Karia, looking around their quaint home.

There was a small fire burning in the fire hole, with some tea brewing for the evening meal. Mim was dressed in a long woven dress, layered with the cotton apron she always wore when preparing meals and herbs. The wall closest to the fire hole was lined with rough wooden shelves that held wooden bowls and baskets filled with herbs.

"He has gone hunting for the evening meal. He should be back shortly. Why do you ask? Did something happen?" Mim questioned.

Juna looked at Karia, wondering if Mim was also aware of the scent. Karia quickly shook her head, motioning Juna to stop his worrying, aware that Mim did always seem able to sense when Karia and Juna had something to talk about.

"We need to speak to the both of you together," Karia told her.

Just then, they heard Sire Argus' hawk approach. Traegons have always used birds of prey as their form of transportation while hunting. Sire Argus entered carrying a sack containing their evening meal. His presence always commanded respect. He laid the sack next to the fire hole, kissed Mim on the cheek, and turned to Karia and Juna. "Good evening, younglings, the hunt went well. We now have enough meat for several days to come. All of you had a good day as well, I presume?"

Dino C. Crisanti

Karia and Juna's Home

"Argus, the young ones have something important they wish to discuss with us," Mim interjected.

"Sit then and we shall speak for a while before our meal," Argus replied, motioning them all to sit around the fire hole. They all sat down and Mim began making preparations for the meal. Sire Argus and Mim gazed at Karia and Juna attentively.

"Go on," Sire Argus prodded.

"When we were in the forest gathering the bark for Mim's tea, we met someone," Karia paused. "A child," Brushing the dirt floor with her hand, she continued, "The one we met was not a Traegon child, but a human child."

Karia and Juna looked timidly at Sire Argus and Mim. They looked at each other and Sire Argus began to breathe heavily. Juna was sure that they were going to be in great trouble, and was having second thoughts about telling them at all. But it was too late.

Finally, with a stern look in his eye, Sire Argus spoke in a deep and angry tone. "Do you two have any idea what you have done, and what this could mean for the entire Traegon race? Have we not made it clear to you that contact of any kind with humans could destroy our kind? They will come looking for us now, and we will have to leave our home. The entire community will be forced out. What you have done is unthinkable! How could you be so careless?" He took a deep breath and stretched his neck and back.

"With respect, Sire, may I continue to share the entire tale with you?" asked Karia quietly.

"Proceed then," growled Sire Argus, breathing heavily in an attempt to contain his anger.

"The boy, his name is Dino. We watched him for a long time and when he fell asleep, we investigated him. His mim was calling after him and she wouldn't find him, as he had covered himself in leaves. We were just trying to help him. He left with his mim and then he returned. This time, he watched us. He didn't try to catch us or harm us in any way. I sensed that his intentions were harmless and I approached him and spoke with him."

"I didn't think it was a good idea from the beginning. I had nothing to do with the meeting, I was against it from the start," Juna piped in, hoping for a lighter punishment.

Karia shot Juna an annoyed look and then continued, "He was kind and we spoke for a long while. We shared food and even traded a crystal for this charm." Karia held out her hand revealing the tiny dolphin he had given her. Then she continued, "I explained that he must not speak of our meeting or it could endanger us and our kind. He stated that he understood, and promised not to reveal us to anyone. I truly feel that he is a special child. Do not the Wayseers speak of a human child helping the Traegons?" Karia finished and looked intently at Mim and Sire Argus.

"It is clear to me that you meant no harm to our kind. I commend you for your willingness to assist another in need. Though you should have come to us for guidance prior to revealing yourself to a human, child or not, I do trust in your instincts and hope that you are correct," Mim said in an understanding way.

Sire Argus sat quietly in deep thought, looking concerned before he spoke. "Well, what is done cannot be undone. I believe that the best thing for us to do now is to bring this before Oracle Balstar for further guidance. We shall set out to see him at sun up. Now, let us finish with the preparation of the meal so that we may eat and get some much-needed rest. It seems that the day has been long, and tomorrow looks to be even longer."

Chapter 4
The Missing Charm

On our ride home, my dad asked how we enjoyed our day out. Mom explained how she really enjoyed relaxing and reading. When it was my turn, I told them that I really enjoyed exploring in the woods.

Mom reached into the back seat and told me, "I'll take my watch back now, please." My heart sank as I remembered that I had given the charm to Karia because I was sure that my mother would notice. I took the watch off and handed it to my mother. She placed it on her wrist and then gasped. "Oh no, my dolphin charm, it's gone! Dino, do you know what happened to it?"

I hated to lie to my mom, but I knew that I couldn't tell her what really happened.

"It must have come off when I was in the woods. I'm really sorry, Mom."

Dad reached over and touched Mom's arm. "I'm sure that we will be able to get another charm, Anna, and I'm also sure that Dino won't mind doing a few extra chores to make up for losing it. Right, son?" He looked at me through the rear view mirror.

"No, I won't mind," I responded solemnly.

I sat back in the seat, watching out the window. I felt in my pocket for the crystal, took it out, and looked at it again. It felt smooth and the colors made it look really pretty. I thought about giving it to my mom because I felt really bad about giving away her charm. When I looked up, she was looking back over the seat at me. "What's that you have?" she asked.

"Um, it's a stone, I found it in the woods," I answered.

"It's quite beautiful. May I see it?" I handed the crystal to her.

"This is no ordinary stone, Dino, this is a crystal and a very different one at that. Do you see the rainbow inside?"

I wanted to tell her what Karia had said about it not being a rainbow, but I thought it best not to.

"Yes, Mom, I saw it. Would you like to have it? I'm really sorry about your charm."

She looked at me and smiled. "Absolutely not! This is yours and I think you should hold on to it. I will get another charm, right Jack?" she confirmed, glancing at my dad.

"Right, Anna dear," he responded.

Mom rolled the crystal around in her hand before handing it back to me. "It has a good feeling about it."

I looked at her face and she was smiling again, the same way she had smiled in the woods. I wondered what she was thinking, I wondered what she knew. I didn't want to ask her though, and I didn't want her to ask me anything either.

"I thought so too," I said simply.

She turned back around and I returned to watching out the window.

For the rest of the ride home, I thought about how long it was until next weekend. I would go to school and come home every day. I would do my homework and my chores, just as I had all the days before. But now things seemed different. All of my thoughts were focused on Karia and Juna. I kept going over our conversation in my head; more and more questions kept popping into my mind, things I should have asked. There were so many things I wanted to know about them. I decided I should start keeping a journal with me all the time so I could write down all of the questions I had and be sure I wouldn't forget to ask Karia the next time I saw her. I would have to be careful with it though, so that no one would find it. I thought about where I could keep it. I decided that I would keep it in my jacket pocket whenever I was away from home, and when I was home I would keep it under the mattress of my bed. I would have to make sure to push it way back so that it wouldn't fall out accidentally.

I figured it wouldn't be too hard to keep my journal a secret, or to keep my promise to Karia. Now I just wanted to get home to start my journal. I kept thinking about more and more things I could write. Not only could I write the questions I wanted to ask, but I could also write about my adventures, about Karia and Juna, imagining what they might be doing all week until we next met. In my wildest dreams, I could not have imagined what was really going on.

Chapter 5
The Prophecy Unfolds

As the sun rose to bring a new day upon Traegonia, Sire Argus, Mim, Karia, and Juna prepared for their visit to see Oracle Balstar. Juna assisted Sire Argus in saddling their wild turkey and hooking the family wagon to the back. Karia helped Mim pack the food for the journey, and prepare the gift to be given to Oracle Balstar. It was very early and none had slept well. Little was said while they worked, only what was needed to be said in their preparations to leave. They loaded the wagon, bade farewell to Miracle, and set off in silence.

Shortly into the journey, a dragonfly with large emerald green eyes swooped down and circled the wagon. The turkey came to a stop. Sire Argus pulled a rolled paper from his bag and handed it to the dragonfly. The dragonfly's wings buzzed loudly and he flew off as quickly as he had come.

"What was that paper?" Juna asked.

"The dragonfly is the messenger to the Oracle. When one has intent to visit with the Oracle, the dragonfly senses this and goes to bring the announcement of the forthcoming visit and its purpose," Sire Argus explained.

"How does the dragonfly know who wishes to visit?" Juna inquired, sounding as if he had many more questions to come.

"They just know, Juna, they just know," said Sire Argus, ending Juna's questions.

The journey seemed long and somewhat uneventful. But when they reached the home of the Oracle, it was clear that this was a very special and magical place. They saw a giant weeping willow tree in the distance, the sun was glistening off its long flowing leaves, which reached all the way to the ground. The willow was surrounded by many other huge trees spreading unending into the great forest. This was the main village of Traegonia, and each tree was home to a Traegon family. The commoners generally lived out away from the main village, as Karia and Juna's family did. The village was home to the Oracle, the Sentinels, the Unpuzzliers, and the Well Born. Karia and Juna were in awe of the village, for they had not seen it before, or at least not that they could remember. Most commoner young did not come to the village until they were ready to take their place as active members of the community.

As the wagon approached the willow tree, Karia noticed the dragonfly that they had seen earlier, flying in and out of the curtain of leaves. It flew down and hung close to the ground, directly in front of them. The wagon came to a stop in front of the dragonfly. Moments later, two Sentinels pulled back the curtain of leaves and motioned them to enter. They all climbed out of the wagon and a squire appeared to lead the turkey and wagon away. One would have thought it to be dark inside, but the sun, poured through in streams of light, glistening and reflecting off of the leaves. There was a small waterfall that ran into a pond near where they entered. The pond held many fish of every color imaginable, and lily pads floated across the top. There were ferns and flowers growing neatly, and vines climbing the trunk of the tree. Scattered about were small wooden benches where one could sit and rest.

The Sentinels directed the family to wait in the garden for further instruction. Mim and Sire Argus took a seat on a bench near the pond, admiring the gracefulness of the fish and the beauty all around. Karia and Juna walked around in awe of the elegance and artistry of the garden, as they had never seen anything like this place before. Mim gave them specific instruction not to touch anything, and to remain close in case they were called upon. As they walked, they were amazed by the peacefulness. They listened to the song chimes hanging from different places way up in the tree, moving with the warm soft breeze. There were crystals of all different sizes everywhere. They were so clear that they seemed to glow in the sunlight.

Suddenly, a robed hooded figure seemed to just appear from out of the trunk of the tree. His robe was woven of hide and cotton, and his hood was a deep royal red color. He wore a pouch on his right hip, a bag over his left shoulder, and he carried a large, crooked walking cane.

"I am Master Zoal, Keeper of all things known. Please follow me, as Oracle Balstar is ready to see you now."

A door appeared in the trunk of the tree behind him, he turned and stepped through as Karia and her family followed. They were led into a spiral staircase carved up through the center of the tree into a Great Room. There were four wooden chairs set in the center of the room, and another off in the back corner by a small writing desk with only a quill pen on top. Master Zoal immediately walked to the back and took his place at the desk, pulling a rolled paper from his bag. In one corner near a window was a large table with many glass bottles. There were herbs, stones, writing paper, and a crystal ball in the center. Mim was particularly intrigued. An impressive chair stood at the head of the room and an even more impressive Traegon was sitting in the chair. His robe and hood were a deep forest green speckled with many tiny crystals sewn onto it, which sparkled in the darkness of the room. He wore a stone on a chain around his neck and an old, beautiful key dangled from his belt. His white hair was a stark contrast against his dark hood. He was quite old and used a crooked cane to assist him to his feet. He moved slowly to greet the family, his kind eyes blinked as he began to speak.

"Ah, Argus and Alistia! It has been a long while since I have seen you, not since your younglings were new. I do hope you have all been well." Oracle Balstar spoke in a low warm voice.

"It is good to see you as well, Oracle. I wish it was under better circumstances, though," expressed Sire Argus.

"I am not worried, Argus, a youngling of yours must have had good reason to make herself known to a human." He glanced over at Karia. "I know that you and Alistia have worked hard at raising your young in a good way. Please make yourselves comfortable. Let us speak for a while." Oracle Balstar returned to his chair and motioned for the rest of them to sit as well. "Now, Karia, brave one, please come forward and share with me your tale."

Karia was nervous and glanced at Mim and Sire Argus. She was surprised that Oracle Balstar already knew about the boy. Argus nodded and Mim held out a bundle for Karia to gift to Oracle Balstar. Karia took the bundle and walked timidly before Oracle Balstar. She knelt down on one knee and handed the bundle to him. He took it graciously and patted Karia on the head. Karia sat before him and began her story.

She told him all about meeting the boy and their visit. She told him about the trade, crystal for charm. He listened intently. There was no expression on his face the entire time she was speaking, just an occasional blinking of his warm eyes. Finally, her tale was finished. There was a long silence. Master Zoal cleared his throat from the back of the room. Oracle Balstar looked up, saw Master Zoal holding up a scroll, and Oracle Balstar nodded. Zoal walked to the front of the room and handed the scroll to Balstar. All eyes were fixed on Oracle Balstar as he slowly unrolled the old yellowed paper. He took a deep breath and read.

"Let it be known: When the talisman meets the stone,
impending peril looms.
Embrace the young one who is dissimilar,
and put the white seed to task,
To open the portal that will bring promise.
The young amass purity of courage
and the sunbow is forever hope."

There was silence in the room. Oracle Balstar looked up from the scroll and over at Karia.

"Do you understand what this prophecy means, youngling?" he asked her.

"I think it seems to be saying that Dino and I were meant to meet, is that correct?" she asked.

"Yes, but it also foretells of much more. If it is true that this prophecy is beginning, Traegonia may be headed into a state of darkness, of danger to us all," Oracle Balstar clarified.

"I did not mean to bring harm to our kind, Oracle," Karia began.

"It is not you who has done anything. This had been laid out as our future many, many years ago. It only means that if this boy is "the one," then you and this boy will have some serious work before you. We must first determine if this is the beginning of the prophecy. There is much to do for you and I. Do you think that you are up to such an undertaking as this?" Oracle Balstar prodded.

Karia's eyes widened. She glanced back at Mim and Argus, and they nodded in approval.

"This is a great deal of information to understand. I fear, of course, for Traegonia, but I am also excited at the possibility of being able to assist our community," she spoke slowly, pausing to think and then continued. "I guess there is no question of what I must do, I will do my very best to honor this prophecy and my family. Whatever is required of me, I will do. Thank you."

"And so, it is stated. Thank you, young Karia," Oracle Balstar announced. He invited the family to remain in the village overnight, and informed them that a meeting of the community elders would be held first thing the following day, and that further instruction would be forthcoming.

A Sentinel appeared at the doorway. "I am Nintar," he told the family. "Come with me and I will show you to your quarters."

He turned and Argus, Mim, Karia, and Juna stood and followed him. They were all quite curious as to where they would be staying that night. They followed Nintar down the wooden stairway and back into the garden, then around to the backside of the large willow, where giant roots rolled from the ground. Small lanterns were hung at various places along them. With the dim light reflecting off of the roots, it created an appearance of mighty snakes intertwining. Each arch in the root held its own doorway, leading into the earth beneath. Argus and his family were motioned to one of the doorways. Nintar pushed open the door, bowed his head, turned, and left. Sire Argus pushed the door open further and they all entered in behind him.

The room was large, charming, and inviting. Candle lanterns flickered and lit the room well. All of the furniture was carefully handmade of narrow twisted roots, bound together to form beautiful ornate pieces. There were two beds, each made for just one, placed in the back of the room separated by a small table with a lantern on top. On the opposite side, there was one large bed for Mim and Sire Argus. Both of the sleeping areas were separated from the rest of the room by woven willow screens. Each bed was crowned with a twisted willow root headboard, and the sleeping mat was made from woven willow whips, with all of the leaves still attached. The blankets that were laid across the foot of each bed were made from thick woven cotton. There was a complete meal laid out upon a large table, surrounded by four chairs.

Seeing and smelling the array of food, the family realized then that they were quite hungry and sat down around the table. They took a moment to admire the food and gave thanks for it and their safe journey. The meal was grand: hot cattail soup, a rabbit roast with roasted wild onions and wild carrots, tender mullen root, and crabapple wine for Sire Argus and Mim.

"This place is wonderful," Karia marveled. "And the food is better than any I have had before."

Sire Argus looked at Mim and smiled.

"This food isn't near as good as you make, Mim. Yours is the best anywhere," retorted Juna quickly.

"I did not mean it that way, Mim. You do make very fine meals as well," Karia jumped in, shooting an angry look at Juna.

"I know what you meant, Karia. The food here is very wonderful and this room, well, it seems fit for royalty. You two should enjoy this while you have the chance. Never before have Sire Argus or I had the opportunity to stay in a place such as this."

"You are quite right, Alistia, and you two had better act in a way befitting such a place. We will most likely be introduced to some of the highest elders in the community, and I will not have you acting like two bickering badger young," said Argus. "This is a very important matter. This is something that most Traegon younglings only dream of. Do you both understand what I am telling you?"

"Yes, Sire," Karia and Juna responded in unison.

They continued to eat their meal and then for the remainder of the evening played cricket; an ancient game consisting of racing crickets through a carved wooden maze.

Very early the next morning, before the sun rose, there was a knock on the door. Sire Argus answered and Nintar gave him the instructions.

"You are requested to attend the meeting of elders to be held at the oldest Black Oak at the northeastern end of the village, precisely as the sun rises over the eastern hills. Specific directions will be awaiting you in your wagon." Nintar bowed and left.

They dressed immediately and headed out to attend the meeting. When they exited the willow curtain, they saw their turkey and wagon were already waiting. They all climbed into the wagon and set off. Even though it was very early, there were many Traegons about the village. The directions brought them through Mazus Grove, the main village marketplace. Mazus Grove was where many Traegons would come very early in the morning to trade their wares. They traded items they had made, like furniture and clothing, food that they grew for the villagers, herbs and medicines, and stones and crystals. The marketplace would open very early before sunup each morning. Traegons would bring their wares in wagons pulled by tamed rabbits, squirrels, and sometimes even turtles and they would line the outer edges of the grove. Stone fire holes were set next to each wagon to offer light to the traders. The visiting patrons carried small lanterns with crude-looking candles. Stalks of small blue flowers rose up from behind the vendors, adding a lovely backdrop to the surroundings. The market closes within hours of the sun coming up. So many Traegons in one place would make it too easy to be discovered in daylight hours.

As they drove through Mazus Grove, Sire Argus spotted an old friend. The wagon came to a stop and a strong looking he-Traegon approached.

"Arbalest Bendbow," Sire Argus called, extending his hand.

"Argus, my friend, it is good to see you and your family. Alistia, you are a vision as always, and look at your younglings, growing them good and strong, I see."

"Thank you for your kind words, Arbalest," said Sire Argus. "Where are you off to on this fine day?"

"I have been called in by the elders for a new assignment. I am heading over to an elders meeting now," answered Arbalest.

Argus looked at Alistia and back at Arbalest. "It seems that we are headed in the same direction. Would you like to rest your feet the remainder of the way?"

"You are headed to the Black Oak?" Arbalest questioned in a surprised tone.

"Yes," Argus responded, not wanting to offer any other information.

"Thank you, I do believe that I will take you up on your offer," said Arbalest, understanding Argus' willingness to end the discussion. He climbed in and they continued on.

Beyond Mazus Grove lay a field of Royal Fern that led to a large bog. Across the bog in the distance, a silhouette of a large old black oak could be seen against the eastern hills. Orange light glowed from behind the hills, like a candle. As the wagon rounded the bog, a large stone fire hole could be seen at the entrance to the oak, where two Sentinels stood guard. The sweet smell of burning cedar filled the air as they approached. They pulled their wagon into a field where other wagons were standing, and secured their turkey. Together, they walked to the entrance of the Black Oak. One of the Sentinels spoke in a direct and emotionless tone. "Name?"

"Arbalest Bendbow," Arbalest stated.

The other Sentinel opened a rolled paper and scanned it for a match. He nodded to the first Sentinel, who told him, "You may enter. Names?" he promptly asked again, looking at Argus.

"Argus, Alistia, Karia, and Juna Banal." Argus said to the Sentinel. Again, the Sentinel scanned the rolled paper; they watched in anticipation as if they might not be on the list. Finally, the nod came and they were ordered to enter.

Inside the Black Oak, they followed others down a long winding corridor to a very large room. There were six chairs that stood behind an old, long, ornately carved wooden table at the head of the room. To the right of the table was another chair. This one was larger with many ornate carvings on the arms and back. To the left of the table was a writing desk and chair, just like the one they had seen at the old willow. There were many other chairs placed in rows, facing the table at the head of the room. Traegons, much older than Argus and Alistia, were standing around talking in a low tone. There were absolutely no other younglings there except for Karia and Juna.

When the foursome walked into the room led by Arbalest, all eyes were fixed on Karia and Juna. The two young Traegons felt very uncomfortable being the center of the strangers' attention. A chime sounded from outside the old oak and at almost that exact moment, a stream of sunlight broke through the window, showering the long table in a warm golden glow. All of the Traegons began to take their seats as did Argus, Alistia, Karia, and Juna. Master Zoal entered the room followed by Oracle Balstar. They took their places; Zoal at the writing desk and Balstar in the large ornate chair.

Moments later, six distinguished older Traegons entered. These were obviously the panel of elders, and everyone was respectfully quiet. There were three she-Traegon and three he-Traegon elders. They took their seats at the long table and looked out upon the room. Oracle Balstar stood and spoke.

"The Court of Elders is now in session. All will remain seated until spoken to. If one wishes to address the panel without being directed, you may do so by tapping your cane two times upon the floor, at which time you will be allowed to speak."

That statement prompted Juna to look back around the room. Many of the Traegons carried their own walking canes.

But what about those who don't have canes, he thought, thinking of Sire Argus and Mim.

"Anyone without a cane may, at this time, proceed to the back of the room where there are additional canes that you may use for the duration of the meeting," Oracle Balstar continued, answering Juna's unspoken question. "Speaking out of turn will result in your being removed from this meeting."

Balstar paused to allow those without canes time to secure one. A few Traegons including Argus and Alistia went to the back of the room to retrieve a cane for the meeting and then returned to their seats. Juna and Karia remained seated.

"Presiding over this meeting, the panel of elders is: Madam Shoran, Sir Antar, Sir Gortho, Madam Calthia, Sir Pexor, and Madam Taendia. We have come before the court to decide the course of action in the matter of the Sunbow Prophecy. I call Karia Banal before the court."

Karia stood and timidly walked forward. She was very uneasy about being alone in front of all of these strangers. She was instructed to tell the panel her tale and she did so. Everyone was quiet as she spoke. When she concluded, there was a pause and then two loud taps upon the floor from the back of the room, breaking the silence. Oracle Balstar stood. "You may speak," he stated.

A very old, angry-looking Traegon stood up in the last row of seats. In a very loud and agitated voice, he called out, "This is an atrocity! Traegons everywhere have been pushed out of the vast lands that we once occupied. Our Traegon brothers of the sands and those who live near the fog, the ones who dwell in the warm lands and those of the mountains, they have all been forced into the tiniest patches of land that have not yet been taken over by these humans. Even the Traegons of the coldest areas are beginning to lose parts of their Traegonia boundaries. Who does this young one think she is to even speak to a human? In all of my days in Traegonia, I have never encountered such a misbehaved, disrespectful Traegon young. She should be locked away so as not to bring any further danger to our community!"

Karia shrunk in front of the elders. Sire Argus looked as if he would attack the speaker, like a lion protecting his young. Mim held tightly to his arm. Before the old one could even finish his sentence, a thunder of pounding canes erupted in the room. Karia was unsure and fearful of what would happen next. Suddenly, Sir Gortho stood and slammed his cane on the long table. "Silence!" he called in a stern voice then continued as the room fell silent. "Sir Dour, there is no need for this infuriation. I am completely confident that this young one meant no harm to our community. And the harshness of your tone is surely not needed here. Are you denying the existence of the Sunbow Prophecy?"

"The Prophecy that is spoken of, how can you be sure that it addresses this particular situation? If you have any doubt, if you are not completely sure, it could bring devastation to our very existence," responded Dour.

"That, Sir Dour, is exactly why we are here, to determine if this human is the one the prophecy speaks of. Now kindly take your seat and please contain your anger. You have frightened this youngling," Gortho reprimanded, motioning toward Karia.

"Now," Gortho continued, "it seems to me that there is a good possibility that this boy just might be the one the prophecy speaks of. Is this agreed upon by the court?" Gortho looked to the panel of elders and to Oracle Balstar.

Each member of the panel nodded, as did Oracle Balstar. Madam Shoran stood. Her eyes were deeply kind, though her presence was strong. "I believe it is of great importance that we protect the younglings while we make our determination of the intentions of the human. I am very aware that she and her brother will need to take part in the effort, but as their elders, it is our responsibility to ensure their safety."

"I agree." Sir Antar stood as Madam Shoran sat back down. "I have called upon Arbalest Bendbow to follow closely. He will ensure that Karia and Juna are not placed in harm's way."

Sir Gortho stood again. "Is it agreed upon that Bendbow should be the one to watch over these younglings?"

The panel of elders all nodded in agreement. Argus was most agreeable to this, and also relieved; he and Arbalest had been as close as brothers from the time they were very young, so he knew that Arbalest would watch over his young as he himself would.

"Now then, our last order of business shall be to resolve how it is that we will determine whether this boy is whom we believe him to be," Gortho proceeded.

Oracle Balstar tapped his crooked cane upon the floor and brought himself to a slow stand. "I believe the prophecy itself answers this." He reached into his hide bag and pulled out a folded cloth. Before he opened it, he recited a portion of the prophecy. "Embrace the young one who is dissimilar and put the white seed to task."

He unfolded the cloth revealing a white acorn. When the light from the sun hit it, it glistened.

"This is how we will determine the boy's worthiness. This is an ancient acorn that grew on this very tree during its first growing season. All of the acorns produced by this tree were black except for this one, and there has not been another one since. The Oracle who held this seat at that time had a vision just before this acorn grew. His vision bore the Sunbow Prophecy. This acorn and this prophecy have been with this Traegon community ever since. Karia should give it to the boy and instruct him to place it beneath his pillow at the end of each day. We should then be able to communicate with him, if, of course, he is the one. If so, he will be able to travel through his dreams into our world, and if he is not, Karia will regain possession of the seed and there will be no more communication with the boy, ever."

"And it is that simple?" questioned Antar.

"Yes, it really is that simple. The power beheld by this seed is truly a gift. If the boy is not the one, he will not have any interest in the acorn and gladly return it to Karia. What will be interesting is if we are able to communicate with him initially. We then will have to take the next steps in our determination, but we will at least be assured of our ability to trust him. Many, many moons ago, we believed that we had found the prophesied child. We know that the process works. My instincts also tell me that this time may somehow be connected to that time as well, but in what way, I cannot yet be sure."

Everything had been agreed upon and the rest of the community was asked to wait and trust in their court to make the correct decisions. A meeting would be called at a later time to apprise the community of any news. The court was adjourned and Karia was entrusted with the white acorn.

Chapter 6
Taking Responsibility

I have to say that getting back to my everyday life was even tougher than I had thought it would be. I mean it was only one day, but it was probably the greatest day of my life. I had never really had any trouble in school before, but now I found myself doodling in my journal, and daydreaming when I should have been listening in class.

On the first day back, when the teacher called on me to answer a question, I couldn't answer it. Not because I didn't know the answer, but because I hadn't heard the question. When we had quiet reading time, I stared at my book as my mind wandered back to the forest.

What will next weekend be like? Will I even see them again? I thought to myself.

Suddenly, the bell rang and reading time was over. The morning had just flown by and now it was lunchtime. Because of the warm weather, we were allowed to go outside to eat. I took my lunch and went over to a shady area under a big tree, away from the rest of the kids. As I ate, I drew in my journal, trying hard to remember every detail about Karia. I drew her face first. She was thinner than Juna, though slightly taller, and her jaw wasn't as square as his. She was pretty though, in her own way. Her personality was strong and direct, I had never met any girl who seemed so sure of herself, and so unafraid of the unknown.

She wore two different earrings. One was a half moon and the other some sort of circle, maybe it was supposed to be a sun. She wore a scarf around her neck and a necklace that looked more like a sun than the earring did. The vest she wore over her dress was made of some sort of hide, laced up the front, and she had a long beaded belt wrapped around her waist. Strange as it seemed, she somehow looked perfectly normal to me.

"Hey, whatcha doin?" a voice startled me from behind.

I slammed my journal shut fast, as my heart raced even faster. "Geeze, Quinn, don't sneak up on me like that! You want to give me a heart attack?"

Quinn was one of my closest friends. We had known each other since kindergarten. He was a small boy, much smaller than me. He had blonde curly hair that his mother let him grow out because she liked the way the curls looked. He was a really nice kid, but he had this bad habit of sneaking up on you without any warning. He was able to be really quiet when he wanted to, and then really loud when he was right behind you. Quinn laughed after he realized he had scared me half to death.

"What are you drawing? It looked pretty weird." I didn't know how long he had been standing there watching me so I didn't know how much he saw.

"I'm just doodling, it's nothing. What are you doing?" I asked turning the question back to him, in the hope that he wouldn't ask any more about my drawing.

"I just finished lunch. I was looking for you to eat lunch with you. I thought maybe you went home or something. Why are you sitting all the way over here? Don't ya like me anymore?" he asked, smiling.

"No, that's not it. I just felt like sitting by myself today. Is that alright?" I snapped before I could stop myself.

Dino C. Crisanti

Karia

Quinn's eyes widened and he stepped back. "What's wrong with you?"

"I'm sorry, Quinn. I didn't mean to say it like that…"

Just then the bell rang, lunch was over. *Saved by the bell,* I thought to myself. We walked back to class, neither of us saying a word. Now instead of daydreaming about Karia and Juna, I was feeling like a jerk for the way I acted toward Quinn. But I didn't think he should be looking at my stuff without asking and I couldn't let him find anything else out. I guess I would just have to be a lot more careful with my journal.

"I hope you're in a better mood after school," Quinn broke into my thoughts just as we reached the classroom. "Do you want to ride bikes after school?"

"Um, I can't today, but we can walk home together if you want," I answered.

"Okay, are you sure you're not mad at me?" Quinn asked again.

"Yeah, I'm sure. I just have some things to do for my mom today. Maybe we can ride bikes tomorrow," I told him, remembering that I had extra chores to do.

We went back to class. I really didn't think it was going to be this hard to keep this secret. I really felt bad for the way I treated Quinn because he's a really nice kid and a good friend. I wished I could tell him, I think he would like Karia and Juna. But I couldn't tell anyone, not even Quinn. I would just have to make time to spend with him, between my chores and school and writing and daydreaming. I didn't want him to suspect anything, and I sure didn't want to keep hurting his feelings.

When school was over, I met Quinn and we walked home together. I apologized to him again for the way I acted earlier. I told him that I had lost my mom's charm and that's why I couldn't ride bikes today. I think he was okay after we talked.

When I got home, I went straight to my room. Mom was out in the yard doing some gardening, and she hadn't seen me come in. Up in my room, I pulled an old wooden box out from under my bed. My dad had given it to me on my sixth birthday. It had belonged to his father, who also gave it to him when he was six. I've always kept different things in it that I thought were special. This had seemed the perfect place to keep the crystal that Karia had given to me. I opened the box and carefully removed the crystal. I polished it with my shirt and set it on my dresser. I sat for a while admiring it from my bed. As I was staring at it, it began to glow and the rainbow started to shimmer. Just then, my mom called, startling me.

She must have seen my book bag, I thought to myself. "Coming, Mom." I quickly put the crystal back into the box and shoved it under my bed. I pulled my journal from my jacket pocket and pushed it far under my mattress. As I hurried down the stairs, Mom was waiting for me at the bottom.

"You don't come and say hello to me anymore?" she asked, kind of disappointed.

I usually came home and found her right away to tell her how my day was. It was like our time together.

"Sorry, Mom," I replied.

"Come out to the garden with me and tell me about your day," she said, turning and walking back outside.

I followed quietly, thinking about the crystal and how strange the glowing was.

"Anything interesting happen at school today?" she asked, putting her gloves back on.

"No, not really, just the same old school stuff. Do you have any extra chores for me to do? You know, because of your charm."

"You don't have much to say today. Is everything alright?" Mom asked, looking up from the ground at me.

"No, Mom, everything is fine. I just want to get my chores done so I can ride bikes with Quinn tomorrow."

"How is Quinn, anyway?"

"He's fine, he just wanted to hang out today, but I told him I couldn't, maybe tomorrow. So can I do my chores now?"

"Alright, I suppose you can start by picking up the branches and leaves from where I pruned the bushes, and then you can go on and do your other chores." She pointed to all of the branches and leaves strewn around the yard.

I started picking up the leaves and putting them into a large brown paper yard bag. My hands were getting sticky from the sap where the branches had been cut. I held a piece and looked at the end. I remembered how Karia and Juna had treated the tree when they took the bark in the woods. I wondered what their world must be like. I finished cleaning up the yard and was just putting out the garbage when my dad pulled into the driveway. He saw me and waved to me to go to him. I walked over and he handed me two small boxes.

"This one is for your mom and this one is for you," he told me.

I looked at him confused.

"Give the blue box to your mom," he continued.

"What's in the other one?" I asked.

"It's a watch. I don't think you should borrow your mother's anymore. Have you been doing any extra chores for her today?" he asked.

"Yes, Dad, I came straight home after school to take care of that," I responded.

"Good, now let's go and give that other box to your mom and see what's for dinner," he suggested, as we walked into the house.

Mom was pleased with her new charm and she hooked it on to her watch immediately. I took my watch up to my room and then returned to the kitchen for dinner. We all ate and then I cleaned up the kitchen as another extra chore. Mom and Dad sat on the porch and talked.

When I finished, I went to my room to do my homework. I took the crystal out of the box and placed it on my desk again, while I did my homework. This time, nothing happened, it just sat there. I kept looking up to see if it would change, but nothing happened at all.

When I finished my homework, I went downstairs to say goodnight to my parents then went back to my room and lay on my bed, writing in my journal for a while before working on the picture of Karia. After a while, feeling tired, I put away the crystal and my journal and went to sleep.

The rest of the week went by slowly. Each day, I did a few extra chores and occasionally rode bikes with Quinn. The whole week, I was just waiting for the weekend, waiting to see Karia and Juna again.

Chapter 7
The Perfect Catch

Finally, the weekend was here, I got up early because I was too excited to sleep. Mom was in the kitchen making our lunch for the picnic.

"Good morning, Dino. You're up early. Sit down and have some breakfast. Your father is out getting his fishing gear together."

"What time are we leaving?" I asked, trying not to sound too anxious.

"Well, since you're up so early, I suppose we can go as soon as we have everything together."

Dad walked through the door. "Well, are we almost ready? Maybe we can get out there before the fish have had their breakfast," he chuckled.

"I'm ready," I announced.

"Well then, put the basket and cooler in the car and we can hit the road," Mom told me.

I jumped up from the table and finished putting the stuff in the car. Mom straightened up the kitchen and we headed out.

It was a cool morning and the birds were chirping. The air smelled very clean. I stared out the car window in anticipation. Finally, we pulled into the clearing near the forest where we always parked. There were never a lot of people here and I think that's why my parents liked it so much. I helped my mom and dad unload the car and set up our picnic spot. Dad grabbed his gear and headed down the hill toward the water.

"Wish me luck," he said as he walked away.

"Can I go on my adventure now?" I asked.

"Do you have your watch?" Mom responded sternly.

"Yes, it's right here in my pocket. Can I go?"

"I suppose, but be back around noon for lunch," Mom answered as she made herself comfortable on the blanket with her book.

I walked down the path into the woods. It was cool and there were tiny drops of dew all over the leaves making everything sparkle in the sunlight. When I got close to where I had met Karia and Juna the last time, I began to softly call their names.

"Karia, Juna… Karia, Juna are you here? It's me, Dino." I repeated this over and over again as I walked further and further into the forest. I looked all around, far off in the distance, up in the trees, and behind every bush I passed, calling them over and over again.

"Arbalest, why can I not let him know that we are here?" asked Karia impatiently. "He will think that we did not come."

"Let him come further into the woods. I want to be sure he has not been trailed," Arbalest whispered. "Okay, he is almost where I wish him to be. Now, you two go and speak with him. I will remain nearby. Do not let him know that I am with you. I will be close the entire time. If there is trouble, I will come. Go now."

Karia burst forth, not even waiting for Juna.

"Karia, wait! I am coming with you," reported Juna as he picked up speed.

"Dino!" Karia popped out from behind a tree startling me, Juna following close behind.

"Where have you been?" I asked, catching my breath.

"I apologize, my friend. I heard you, but I just had to wait until you were closer," Karia answered.

"Closer, to what?" I asked.

"We just have to be careful not to be discovered by anyone else," Karia answered. "How was your time away from here? What do you do when you are not in the forest?"

"I have been keeping a journal about our meeting," I confided.

"What is a journal?" Karia asked, relaxing a bit.

I pulled the journal out of my jacket pocket and laid it on the ground in front of Karia. She moved toward it. The journal looked really big as she stood in front of it.

"Go ahead, open it," I told her.

Karia reached to open the journal. Juna moved in close behind her to get a better look. Karia opened the journal to the first page; the writing must have looked like scribble to her because she cocked her head back and forth as she looked over the page. She turned to the second page and Juna let out a gasp.

"That is you, Karia. You are in that book. This is not good. No, this is very bad." Juna shook his head back and forth.

"This is not to be believed," Karia said, as she brushed her hand over the picture of herself. "Did you make this?" she asked, looking up at me.

"Yes, I drew it," I answered.

"And what are all of these lines? Do they mean something?" she asked, moving her hand over the written words.

"This is not good. No, not good at all," Juna was still mumbling.

"Don't you like the picture, Juna?" I asked him.

"Others will find out. They will see this image. They will come looking for us. We must destroy it," Juna said, as he lunged at the journal.

Karia grabbed his arms before he could reach the page. "NO! Juna, you cannot do that." She forcefully turned Juna around and let him go.

"For one thing, this book does not belong to you, and for another, it is very well done."

"Oh, Juna, I promise you I will never show this to anyone. I am keeping it safe, away from everyone. I won't let anyone find it, and I would never let anyone harm you," I tried to explain, trying to calm him down.

It was clear that he still didn't trust me, at least not the way that Karia did. She was still looking closely at the picture and the words written in the journal, seeming not to even hear our conversation.

"These lines, what did you say they were?" she asked again.

"They are words, I am writing about our meetings and I also write down questions I don't want to forget to ask you," I continued.

"What kinds of things do you wish to know?" Karia asked, finally turning her attention from the journal.

"Well, I would really like to know how it is that you are able to just disappear. One minute you are right there in front of my eyes, and then I turn around and you are gone. I wasn't sure if I had seen you at all."

"Where does it say that?" asked Karia, looking back at the journal again.

"Right here," I leaned over to show her where it was written in the journal and read: "Remember to ask Karia how they are able to just disappear the way that they do."

Karia looked at Juna. He was still shaking his head back and forth. "Not now, Karia," he said.

Karia looked back at me. "In time, you shall know the answers to all of your questions. My brother is right, now is not the time."

I nodded in agreement, not really understanding why, now wasn't the right time, and feeling a bit sad that they didn't trust me enough to tell me. I looked down and kicked at the dry leafy dirt.

"Please do not be unhappy, Dino, I promise you that I will tell you in due time," Karia said, sensing my feelings. "I have something else to give to you," she added as she reached into the bag on her hip.

She pulled out a rolled dark cloth and began to open it. She pulled out an acorn and held it out to me. I took it and looked at it very carefully. It was not like any other acorn I had ever seen before, and I have seen lots of them on my adventures. I thought it seemed to glow as I held it. "This is beautiful," I told her. "I have never seen a white acorn before. Where did you find it?"

"Again, Dino, all things will be revealed in time," Karia said. "I want you to keep this until we meet again. Place it under your pillow when you sleep. Let us know if you notice any strange happenings. Do not show it to anyone though. We cannot risk someone taking it away. It is precious to us. Do you understand?"

I looked at it again, rolling it between my fingers and thinking. I looked up and Karia and Juna were staring at me intently. "What do you mean by strange happenings?" I asked.

"Nothing bad, you have no reason for concern. Just remember; if anything happens, let me know about it the next time we meet. Understand?" Karia looked directly into my eyes.

Looking into hers, I felt a perfect calm come over me. I trusted her completely. "Yes, I understand. Can I write these things in my journal?" I asked.

"I think that will be alright if it helps you to remember. But you must be sure that no one finds and reads this journal of yours. That would surely cause great problems for our kind."

"Okay, Karia, I understand I will guard the journal with my life and the acorn too," I reassured her. I thought for another moment. "I don't have anything to give to you. You know, to trade for the acorn."

"Do not worry. It is not sure that you will be able to keep it. If it is determined the next time we meet that you shall hold it longer, then you may give me something," Karia stated.

"Is there anything special that you might want? I don't think I have anything as special as this."

"Can you make another picture, like the one in your journal?" she asked.

"Yes, I can do that, if that is what you want," I responded happily.

"I would greatly enjoy a picture. You have a special gift for this picture making," Karia said, still looking at the picture of herself.

"Maybe you can make a picture of me also," Juna piped in, surprising me a bit, after the commotion he had caused over the drawing of Karia.

"Well, if you would like, I could start one right now," I told him, after checking my watch. "You can just stand or sit right there and I will draw you. Do you want to do that?"

Karia could hardly contain her excitement. "Oh yes, make the picture now. I wish to watch your magic."

I laughed. "It's not magic. I just really like drawing."

I leaned against a nearby tree and opened my journal to a blank page, then pulling a pencil from my jacket pocket, I began to draw. Karia stood next to me, watching in amazement. The time seemed to just slip away. I felt an urge to check my watch again and sure enough it was time to get back for lunch.

"I have to go now, but I will be back in a little while. Will you be here when I get back?" I asked closing my journal and putting my pencil back into my pocket.

"I believe that we shall be able to return later. Just come back to this place and call. We can continue with the picture then," Karia answered.

I stood and walked down the path. "Goodbye for now," I called. I hurried back to the picnic site, so I wouldn't be late. As I came out of the woods, I could see my mom and dad sitting on the blanket together.

As I got closer, I asked. "Why are you back up here from fishing,

Dad?" It seemed strange to me since Mom always took Dad's lunch down to him by the water.

"Not one bite all morning, son. I just don't understand and we were here so early. Usually, that's one of the best times to fish," Dad answered.

"Well, maybe they will bite better after lunch," I said, hoping I was right.

"I hope you are right, son. Otherwise, we might want to try a different spot next weekend."

"Oh, I hope not, Jack" Mom said sadly. "I really like this area. It's so quiet and peaceful."

"Well, we'll just have to wait and see," Dad added, as he took another bite of his sandwich.

As I ate, my mind raced. *What if we don't come back? How will I ever see Karia and Juna again?*

My stomach began to turn and I lost my appetite. *If Dad doesn't catch anything after lunch, we may never come back.* That thought kept repeating itself over and over in my head. *I must tell Karia.* I felt an overwhelming sense of urgency. I choked down as much of my lunch as I could and asked if I could go back out on my adventure.

"I suppose that would be alright," Mom answered, looking at Dad.

"What is it that you do out in the woods for so long?" Dad asked, leaning back on his arms, as if expecting a long answer.

But I didn't feel much like talking about my adventures right now. I just wanted to get back to Karia and Juna. I knew though that if I seemed in a big hurry, they might get suspicious. I glanced back at the opening to the forest.

"I just adventure, you know, climbing trees, following rabbits, chasing squirrels, and just pretending. I pretend all different stuff. It's really fun. I like being in the forest." I tried to make my answer quick.

"Don't you get scared out there all by yourself?" he asked, apparently not noticing that I wanted to go.

"No, it's not scary. Can I go now?" I said.

"I guess so, but be back here by 4:00, we'll be going home around then. Well, I guess I'll go back down and try fishing a little more." Dad sighed.

I stood up and walked slowly back toward the path. As soon as I was out of sight of my parents, I bolted into the forest. When I got back to where I had last seen Karia and Juna, I began calling them. "Karia, Juna. I'm back, are you here? I have to talk to you. Are you here?"

Karia and Juna must have heard my calls and sensed that there was a problem because they appeared as if from out of thin air.

"Dino, here we are." Karia stood in the middle of the path. "What is wrong? Has something happened?"

I tried to catch my breath from running so fast. "My dad," I said puffing.

"Is your father hurt?" Juna asked, with more interest than I had seen from him so far.

"No, it's nothing like that. It's just that he isn't catching any fish, and he said that if he didn't get any bites, then next weekend, we would go somewhere else. We won't be coming back here," I said, still puffing.

"Oh, that is not good, not good at all," Juna replied, looking to Karia for her response.

Being the true warrior that Karia was, she showed no concern. She just looked at me and announced, "Well then, we had better make sure that your father catches something, shouldn't we?"

Juna and I looked at each other puzzled and then back at Karia.

"What do you mean, Karia?" Juna asked suspiciously.

"We are going to need some help and we need to move quickly. We will need to call on Arbalest Bendbow for assistance," Karia replied, very sure of herself.

Juna stared at Karia with wide eyes and then began slowly

shaking his head again. Karia ignored his quiet objection. "Who is Arbalest Bendbow?" I asked.

"He is only the greatest of Traegon hunters," Karia explained.

"Now, be silent. I need to concentrate. Let me attempt to contact him." She opened her arms and looked out into the woods. Juna was still shaking his head back and forth.

"Oh, well, this is quite a feat for a Traegon youngling. I had better pay close attention," mumbled Juna.

Karia began to speak in a melodic tone.

"Oh, Arbalest Bendbow, great Traegon hunter, we are in need of your assistance. If you can hear my voice, please come to our aid."

I scanned the forest but saw nothing. Suddenly, there was movement in the brush nearby and out walked another Traegon. You could tell he was older than Karia and Juna. His clothing was many different colors of green. He wore a cotton cape with a piece of fur that ran down the back. In one ear, he wore the jawbone of some very tiny animal as an earring. He had a coiled rope attached to his belt, and a leather pouch on the opposite side. He carried an archer's bow slung over one shoulder, and a quiver of arrows was poking out from under his cape. He was staring straight at Karia as he walked toward us.

"You called," he said simply, still staring hard at Karia.

"Wow!" It was the only thing I could think to say at that very moment. I even thought I heard Juna chuckle, which was strange coming from him, but when I looked back, he was just standing there still shaking his head.

"What is it that you are in need of, youngling?" Arbalest asked in a strong deep voice and I thought I heard a bit of sarcasm.

"I have a plan that will require your archery skill," Karia began. "Now this is what we shall do."

She explained her plan, which sounded pretty good to me, and then she asked me to lead them to a place just down the river from where my dad was fishing. Arbalest climbed a nearby tree. Karia instructed Juna to remove his belongings and enter the water.

"I will not take part in this. You cannot make me do this, Karia," Juna objected.

"Juna, you must do this. You know that if we do not help Dino, we may never see him again," Karia pleaded, looking into Juna's eyes.

He obviously knew that it was important, even if I didn't know just exactly how important.

"Now, we will swim out beneath the water surface and scout for a fish. It must be a good one. Then we will chase it to the surface, where Arbalest will skillfully lasso it. Then, Juna, you will guide the fish near the hook. I will be waiting and place the hook into the fish. Then we will swim back here and all will be well." Karia laid out the plan.

"And it is that simple, is it?" Juna asked, in a very skeptical tone.

"Yes, it is that simple," Karia responded.

Karia and Juna removed their belongings and slipped into the water. Beneath the surface they searched for just the right fish. Juna pointed to a large blue gill, but Karia motioned that it was not the right one. Karia then spotted a large mouth bass, hanging out in a weed bed near the shore. She motioned to Juna that this was the one. She swam toward it, trying not to scare it too soon. Juna swam around the opposite side to ensure that it would not flee in the wrong direction. From that point, everything happened very quickly.

Noticing them too, the bass swam to the surface and Arbalest took his shot. The arrow, with a lasso attached, swirled through the air, piercing the water and pulling the lasso past the fish. Arbalest quickly pulled back on the rope, catching and securing the fish in the lasso. Juna grabbed for the fish and caught it by the tail. He obviously didn't expect it to be as powerful as it was. He held on with all of his might. The fish was angry now and difficult for Juna to keep control of as it was only slightly smaller than him. Karia swam ahead, she knew that she would have to wait until just the right time before she could grab the hook, or my father might reel her in instead. The bass was moving very fast and Juna was struggling to make his way up toward the lasso. He grabbed the arrow just as Karia grabbed the hook. The hook was in, but Juna was still having trouble freeing the rope. He reached for the arrow, which was still attached to the rope. The bass was putting up the fight of his life. Karia grabbed onto the other end of the arrow and the three of them rolled and turned beneath the surface of the water. They could feel the line pulling them toward the shore, but they couldn't seem to break loose. Suddenly, Juna caught his large feet on a log, wedged in the river floor, and held on. The arrow snapped in two, loosening the rope and allowing the fish to slip free of the loop. Juna and Karia watched as the fish was reeled in.

Karia and Juna swam back to shore. I reached down to help them out of the water. Juna and Karia lay in the brush alongside the water and rested.

"That simple, huh, Karia?" Juna asked sarcastically, trying to catch his breath.

"You should have seen the look on my father's face. I don't think I have ever seen him so excited. Oh, I'm sure he will want to come back here again. You guys did a great job. Thank you, thank you so much."

Arbalest was sitting on a nearby log, closing two hide bags. He stopped and looked up. "I must admit, I am impressed by your labors. Your idea was strong and your efforts are commendable."

Karia looked pleased. "That is a grand compliment, coming from you, Arbalest. I am grateful for your words."

Juna rolled his head to one side, still lying in the brush. "I wish to remain a land creature for the remainder of my existence.

I do believe that if I were meant to be in water, I would have been equipped with more water type parts."

He sat up and began to untangle some seaweed that had managed to get wrapped around one of his ears.

"And look at this tear in my clothing, I am just grateful it was not in me."

"Nonetheless, Juna, your display is most commendable as well," Arbalest told him, picking up one of the bags and tossing it to Karia and Juna.

"Take this home with you. Tell Argus and Alistia that I said you two are deserving of a hunter's meal."

"What is in the bag?" Juna asked.

"While you two were battling the great bass, I took the opportunity to do some fishing of my own," responded Arbalest.

"Fish? You caught fish?" Juna asked, quite amazed. "And you are not even wet. You must show me sometime how to catch the fish without getting wet." He stated, looking annoyed at Karia.

We all laughed. Karia and Juna shook themselves off and recovered their belongings.

"It's getting late, I should probably be getting back to my parents. I had a lot of fun today. I cannot wait until next weekend," I told them reluctantly.

I really didn't want to leave, I wished that I could stay here with them forever.

"I will work on the pictures for you both and bring them next time."

"Do you have the acorn?" Karia asked me.

"Yes, it's right here in my pocket," I replied, feeling in my inside jacket pocket for it.

"Remember what I told you and be sure you do not misplace it," Karia stated in a more serious tone.

"I remember everything that you told me, don't worry. I will take very good care of the acorn," I reassured her. "Well, I'd better go. I'll see you next time. It was nice to meet you, Arbalest. Thank you all, again… for everything."

"Until we meet again," Karia said, bowing her head. Juna raised his hand and bowed his head also.

"It was most enjoyable to meet you, young Dino. I am sure that we will see each other again," said Arbalest.

I turned and walked back to the path. When I looked back, they were still sitting there. I smiled and kept on walking.

When I returned to the picnic site, my mother was packing up. "Dino, you missed it. Your father caught a great big bass. He was so excited, he came up here to show me. I wish you could have been here to see it."

"Does this mean we will be coming back here again?" I asked.

"I would think so. I haven't seen him this excited about a fish in a long time," Mom responded, smiling.

My dad came up the hill carrying his gear and smiling from ear to ear. I ran over to help him.

"Well, son, I've still got it. You should have seen the fish I caught. It was the biggest one I've caught yet. You should have seen it."

"You didn't keep it?" I asked thinking about all the trouble Karia and Juna went to just to help him catch it.

No, son, it's all catch and release here," Dad said. "But I guess we have to come back. Maybe there are even bigger ones than that."

It was settled, we would return to these woods again. I was very happy.

On the ride home, I thought about the acorn and what Karia had told me. I felt for it in my pocket, but didn't dare take it out. I knew my mother would find it interesting but I had promised to keep it a secret. I wondered about the strange things that Karia had mentioned. I had no idea what these things could be. I guess I would just have to wait. When we got back home, I helped my parents un-load the car and then went to take a shower before bed. I took the acorn from my pocket and placed it safely in the box with the crystal. I pushed my journal under my mattress. As I showered, I imagined other pictures I wanted to draw. I imagined what it must have been like for Karia and Juna under the water, the two of them chasing the fish. Arbalest would make a great picture too. He was strong and very interesting.

I dried off and went to my room with these ideas still in my mind. I pulled the box from under my bed and took out the acorn. I placed it under my pillow as Karia had instructed me to do. I was feeling pretty tired, but I wanted to draw for a while. I pulled out my journal and opened to a clean page and began to draw.

Chapter 8
Her World

I must have fallen asleep while I was drawing, because the next thing I remember, I was back in the woods. I was alone and it was dark. I felt frightened. I couldn't see very far and I didn't want to be there. The only thing I could think to do was to call for Karia.

"Karia? Karia, are you here? Can you hear me?"

I heard a rustle in the trees that startled me. I wanted to run but I couldn't see well enough to know which way to go.

"Karia, is that you?" Chills ran down my back. The hair on my arms and on the back of my neck stood on end. I moved over to the nearest tree and crouched down. I closed my eyes in the hopes that I was dreaming and that I would wake up back in my own bed.

"Dino!" I heard a familiar whispery voice say.

I opened my eyes and saw Karia standing in front of me. I grabbed her and hugged her with a deep sense of relief.

"Dino, let go of me. You are squeezing too tight," another whisper came, only this time a little strained.

"I'm sorry, Karia, I was really scared. I'm glad you are here with me in my dream," I responded as I released my grasp on her.

It was at that point that I realized that we were the same size. I stepped back and looked at her. She was even more incredible than I had remembered. She seemed very petite, even though we were seeing eye-to-eye. *Am I her size or is she mine?* I wondered. I couldn't tell in the darkness.

"Yes, I am glad as well. I have some others that I wish for you to meet. We must go now, come follow me," she said.

"Karia, do you realize that we are the same size?" I asked her, since she didn't act as if she noticed.

"Yes, Dino, I know," she responded matter-of-factly. "Now come on, we must go now."

She lit a small candle held within a tin lantern and motioned me to follow. Thanks to the candle, I could see much better, and noticed how big everything looked around me. I knew then that it was I who was her size. The leaves and sticks on the ground were huge compared to my feet. As I walked over the dried leaves, my feet would break through them slowing me down. Karia looked back to see if I was okay. I guess that is why their feet are so big. She didn't seem to have any problems walking across the forest floor. I followed as quickly as I was able. I was watching my own feet as I walked so that I wouldn't fall, and Karia must have stopped because all of a sudden, I bumped hard into the back of her.

"Oh, Karia, I'm so sorry. I wasn't watching where I was going. Are you all right?"

"It is all right, I am fine. We are here now," she answered back.

"Where is here?" I asked her, looking around and seeing only trees.

"This is where I live." She pointed at a large tree standing before us.

As I looked closer, a door appeared in the trunk of the tree and opened slowly. A male Traegon stood in the slightly opened door. He was not very tall, but looked strong for his size. He wore a woven shirt with a tan woven vest on top. He also had long white hair that was pulled back.

"This is Sire Argus. He is to us as your father is to you." Karia explained to me.

"It is nice to meet you, sir. I am Dino," I said introducing myself.

"Yes, I am aware of your name. Come in out of the chilled night air." He pushed the door open further, revealing a flickering light inside.

As I stepped in, I was amazed at how nice and spacious it was being that this was the first time I had been inside a tree.

"This is very nice," I said, looking around.

Then I noticed that there were others sitting in the room as well. They were all sitting around a fire and stood as we entered.

"You already know Juna and Sire Argus," Karia continued her introductions. "This is Mim, she also is to us as your mother is to you. That is Oracle Balstar and Master Zoal."

Each nodded as she stated their names. I was surprised and curious as to why they were all here.

"Come and sit with us, Dino," Mim invited in a soft, kind voice. She was really quite pretty, as far as Traegons go.

I walked across the candlelit room and sat in an open place around the fire. I felt a little out of place, but Mim and Karia did what they could to make me feel welcome.

"Would you like some sage tea?" Mim asked.

"Yes, please," I answered.

I was a little surprised at what she had offered me because my mom also makes sage tea. Mim handed me a carved wooden cup, with steam rising up out of it.

"Thank you," I said, taking a sip.

The warm tea was comforting and made me feel a sense of home. It seemed strange to me, all of it, being inside of a tree, having tea with these strange but wonderful creatures. *What an odd dream I'm having,* I thought. I was sipping the tea and looking around at their interesting home when a deep soft voice spoke.

"What are your feelings for Karia and Juna?" Oracle Balstar spoke directly.

I looked around, confused at the question. "I like them both very much, sir," I responded simply.

"Karia tells me that you and she have been spending much time together, and she feels that you should be considered a trustworthy ally to the Traegons. Do you agree with her assessment?"

I sat quietly thinking about what he was asking me before I responded. "I greatly enjoy the time I have spent with Karia and Juna and have come to understand how important it is that their and your secret remain a secret, and have given them my word that I won't tell anyone about your kind."

Oracle Balstar sat looking at me as I spoke. I wondered if this was what he wanted to know. He blinked slowly and spoke.

"Karia also tells me that you have magic that allows you to create images that you see onto paper. Is this true?"

"It's not magic, sir. As I told Karia, it is just something that I enjoy doing and have become good at. I have always been able to draw different things, ever since I was little. My mom says I have a gift for it," I answered, looking around and thinking about drawing this place.

"May we have a look at these images of yours?" requested Oracle Balstar.

I looked at him and then looked down at myself. I had my jacket on. I felt the outside of my jacket pocket. I didn't remember putting on my jacket, and wasn't sure if I had taken my journal with me but sure enough, it was there in my pocket.

I pulled it out and handed it to Oracle Balstar. He laid my journal on his lap and opened the cover. He turned each page very slowly and very carefully. He motioned to Master Zoal to come and look too. Master Zoal was very interested and excited to see the journal, for not only was he able to write, but he was also able to decipher other writings. He walked around the circle to where Oracle Balstar was sitting and sat down beside him. Balstar slid the journal over to

Master Zoal. He looked closely at the pages. He slowly brushed his hand across the pages and closed his eyes.

I watched curiously as he began to speak. The words that came out of his mouth were my words. He was reading my journal, word for word, without actually looking at the pages. *Now, that is magic,* I thought. When he finished reading, he opened his eyes and looked at each of the pictures.

"These are very well done," he told me, looking up at me.

"Thank you very much. I'm glad that you like them," I answered proudly.

"May we have a look?" Mim asked, directing her question to me.

"Sure," I answered.

"What do you intend on doing with this journal and the things you have written within?" Oracle Balstar asked, as he handed the journal to Mim and Sire Argus.

"I do not plan to do anything with it, sir. It is mine and you all are the only ones who have even seen it. I made a promise to Karia and Juna that I wouldn't show it to anyone, and I plan to keep my promise."

Mim walked around the outside of the circle, reached over my shoulder and handed me my journal. "Your drawings are very beautiful," she told me, placing her hand on my shoulder.

I turned and looked at her. It seemed strange to me that she used the word drawing when everyone else called them pictures or images.

"Thank you," I answered.

"I believe that is all for now," Balstar stated. "Karia, you may take him back now."

I looked around and saw Karia and Juna sitting back away from the circle. Karia stood and walked over to me. I also stood and followed her to the door.

"It was very good to meet you, Dino," Mim called from across the room. "Safe journey," she told me.

"We will speak again," Oracle Balstar declared.

Karia opened the door and we stepped out into the darkness.

The next thing I remember, my mom was calling me.

"Dino, it's time to get up for school. Come on, let's go," she called from the bottom of the stairs.

I got out of bed, went to the bathroom to wash my face, and returned to my room to get dressed. As I buttoned my shirt, I began to remember my dream. Bit by bit, it started coming back. I sat down on my bed and it hit me, the whole thing flooded into my head. It was very clear and seemed so real, but it couldn't have been. *It's impossible,* I thought to myself as I remembered that in the dream, Karia and I were the same size. I stood up and began making my bed. When I moved my pillow, the little white acorn rolled out across my bed.

"Let me know if anything strange happens." Karia's words echoed in my head.

Was this what she was talking about? I wondered, and then my mother's voice broke my train of thought.

"Dino, breakfast is getting cold. Are you just about ready?"

"Coming, Mom," I called back. I picked up the acorn and quickly put it into the box under my bed. I reached under the mattress for my journal. It wasn't there. My heart dropped into my stomach. I looked around my room frantically; under my bed, in my covers, but it wasn't anywhere. I turned around and sat back on my bed, and then I spotted my jacket hanging on the back of my door. I grabbed it and felt the pockets, then let out a huge sigh. It was there. I was relieved but also confused. I knew I had been writing in it last night. I didn't remember putting it back under my mattress, but I know I didn't put it in my jacket either. I finished dressing, went downstairs, ate, and went to school. All the while, I was thinking about my dream, and wondering if it was possible that it was real. I just couldn't be sure until I talked to Karia.

Chapter 9
Leaving Home

When Karia returned home, the group was still sitting around the fire hole talking in very low tones. Juna had already turned in for the night. When Karia entered, they all turned to greet her.

"I am so glad you are back," Mim said, relieved. "I don't like for you to be out in the dark alone, even if it is only a short distance away."

She walked over to Karia, took her wrap and hung it on a wooden rack nearby. "You may sit and talk for a while, but then you must get some rest."

Karia sat at the fire hole and looked at Oracle Balstar.

"Is he the one?" she asked quietly, in a sleepy voice.

"It is highly possible that this is so. But there is more we must do to determine for sure," responded Oracle Balstar. "It will be necessary for you to come and stay at my willow for a while, in order that we might communicate further with the boy. There are many things that you will also learn about your own kind, things that most Traegons do not become aware of until they have aged some. Karia, you must take your place within the community much earlier than expected."

Mim looked at Oracle Balstar and then at Sire Argus with

forlorn eyes. She knew that Karia would be leaving their home, at least for a while.

"Argus, I am not ready for this," Alistia said, trying to choke back the tears she could feel welling up in her eyes. Argus held her arm tight.

"We will stay the night and set out in the morning," stated Oracle Balstar. "Alistia, your young one has an important role to take for the good of all Traegons. You understand this, don't you? She will not be leaving forever, and your family may come for a visit any time you please."

"It is time to get some rest. Karia, you go on to bed. We will discuss more of this at daylight." Argus showed Oracle Balstar and Master Zoal where they would sleep for the night. The room was empty except for Mim and Karia. Alistia sat down next to Karia and placed her arms around her.

"My brave young one, it feels too soon for you to be leaving our home. I never imagined that your place in the community would be so great, or so soon. I will miss you, but I know that you are strong and that you will do well in this endeavor. Know that we are always here for you, my child. We will come and visit as often as we are able."

Karia looked into her Mim's eyes and laid her head upon her shoulder. "You have taught me much, Mim. I know that with the teachings you and Sire Argus have imparted upon me, I will succeed on this journey. I too will miss you and Sire Argus greatly."

Sire Argus quietly entered the room and informed them that it was time to retire for the night. Karia stood and walked over to him. He laid his large hand upon her shoulder, looking at her with warm paternal eyes. "I am quite proud of you, Karia," he told her in a loving tone. "Sleep well."

He motioned her to her room. Mim and Argus retired as well.

The next morning Alistia, Sire Argus, Oracle Balstar, and Master

Zoal were up before the sun had risen. They were sitting by the fire hole drinking tea and eating walnut bread. Their talk was low and muffled. Karia woke and reached over to rouse Juna from his deep sleep.

"Juna, Juna, wake up," Karia whispered as she pushed on Juna's back.

"Augg!" Juna groaned as Karia continued to push at him. "What? What is it that you want, Karia? Go back to sleep! It is much too early to wake yet," Juna mumbled sleepily.

"Wake up, Juna! The rest are already awake and talking about things. Come on! Let's see what they are saying." Karia prodded him again.

"You go on. I wish to sleep some more," Juna said, as he rolled over and covered his head.

Karia got out of bed and walked into the room where they all were sitting. They immediately stopped talking when she entered.

"Good morning, Karia. Are you hungry?" Alistia asked, breaking the uncomfortable silence. "I have some hot walnut mush and fresh walnut bread warming over the fire."

"Yes, please, that sounds very good." Karia sat beside the fire hole. "Good morning, Sire. Good morning, Oracle Balstar. Good morning, Master Zoal," she greeted them all as Mim placed a wooden bowl of piping hot mush before her. They all replied to her greeting.

"Did you sleep well?" asked Oracle Balstar.

"Very well, thank you," she answered.

"That is good, for we will need to leave for the willow soon. Once you have eaten, you shall need to prepare your things," Oracle Balstar informed her.

"I will help Karia prepare her things," said Mim mournfully.

"If we are leaving so soon, we had better wake Juna so that he may also get himself ready," Karia stated with urgency in her voice.

"Juna will not be coming with us, Karia. Only you are needed now." Oracle Balstar spoke quietly as he said this.

Karia looked at Mim and Sire Argus. "Juna is not coming? But we always do everything together."

At that moment, Juna slipped into the room. He had overheard the conversation. He looked at Karia, then at Mim and Sire Argus. They could see the sadness in his eyes.

"I will not be going with you?" Juna asked, hoping that he had heard wrong.

"Not at this time, Juna," responded Oracle Balstar. "The prophecy speaks of only one Traegon young, and clearly this is Karia. She will go on alone from here, at least for now."

Karia and Juna looked at each other. They may have bickered from time to time and disagreed on some things, but they were inseparable.

"I just assumed that Juna would be coming along." Karia focused her statement at everyone in the room.

Alistia walked over to the table where Juna had settled himself and Karia followed.

"All will be fine," she said to the both of them, putting her arm around Juna and her hand on Karia's shoulder. "Everything is as it should be. There is a plan for each of us. And besides, we are not prepared for both of our younglings to leave home so soon. Juna, we need you to stay here. Who will gather my herbs and help Sire Argus with his woodworking? And Miracle would be very, very sad if you both were to leave at once."

Mim searched for the perfect things to say to ease the sadness of her two younglings, while at the same time trying to hide her own. Karia and Juna knew that Mim was right, that things were as they should be. She always told them this when there was no other explanation. But she also turned out to be right all of the time. There always ended up being a reason for things to happen the way that they did.

"Everything will be just fine," she repeated again. "Now, Karia, let us go on and prepare your things for your journey. Argus, would you please prepare Juna his morning meal? I think that he could use something warm in his belly.

Argus prepared Juna's breakfast, and Juna sat quietly at a table near the fire hole. Juna kept trying to make sense of the morning's conversation. But no matter how hard he tried, he couldn't find any good reason in his mind for the decision. He believed what Mim was telling him, but this time it was just harder for him to understand. He and Karia had never been separated before.

A short time later, Karia and Mim emerged from Karia and Juna's room, carrying a large traveling bag with them. Karia was dressed in her traveling clothes. Master Zoal and Oracle Balstar had also gathered their things and prepared their wagon. Juna was not waiting with the others. Karia bade farewell to Sire Argus and Mim. Mim handed her a satchel of homemade treats for her journey. They walked outside where Juna and Miracle were sitting on a tree branch, watching and waiting. They climbed down out of the tree when they saw Karia. Juna stood before her, he looked first at the ground and then at her.

"We will be together again soon. Be safe," he said solemnly.

It was a sad moment but Juna loved Karia very much, and didn't want to make this harder than it already was. He was comforted in knowing that he would at least be staying in a familiar place.

Karia climbed into the back of a large wagon that was being pulled by a large quail. Master Zoal climbed into the front and took the reins. Oracle Balstar climbed in next to Master Zoal. Karia looked back at her family as the wagon began to slowly pull away. Mim, Sire Argus, and Juna all stood watching with their hands out in front of them, palms open toward her as the wagon pulled away. In the Traegon tradition, holding your palms outward was a symbol of wishing safe travel and protection on the travelers' journey. Miracle just shook his tail and quickly disappeared back up into the tree. Karia held her hands out, as if catching all of their good and protective thoughts, then held them to her heart, as the wagon rounded a grove of thistle and disappeared from sight.

Chapter 10
New Surroundings

As the wagon made its long journey through the forest, Karia sat quietly in the back pondering the mornings' events and trying not to feel too sad about leaving her family. She watched the trees go by and listened to the leaves crunching under the wheels of the wagon. It was beginning to get warm and she was feeling a little tired. She lay down in the back of the wagon. She rested on the bags and watched the sky go by.

Suddenly a huge raven, black as night, began to circle the wagon, way up in the sky. Karia watched it for a long while as it gracefully danced in the breeze. With each circle that it made around the wagon, it seemed to be getting lower and lower. Karia thought she was imagining it until it broke through the treetops. Then she realized that it was intentionally staying close to the wagon. She watched as it carefully navigated its way through the branches, not stopping once to rest.

Karia rolled over and called the others, "Oracle Balstar, I believe that we are being watched, and followed for that matter."

"And who, may I ask, is it that is following us, Karia?" he asked.

"A giant raven, sir. He has been following for a while, but now he is getting much closer," Karia answered.

"Now, Karia, if this raven were to mean us harm, do you not

think that you should have spoken of him sooner?" Oracle Balstar asked in a very calm voice that unnerved Karia.

Karia's stomach turned. "Um, I cannot be sure if he means us harm or not. The only experience I have had has been with crows. Juna and I would chase them through the wild strawberry fields. They never tried to harm us though, I don't think, as we thought they were just playing when they would chase us and dive at us. We would run and dive into the brush when they got too close, but they would just holler and fly off."

"Well, it sounds as if you had much enjoyment playing with the crows," Balstar responded.

"Yes, Oracle, we enjoyed this very much," said Karia, already missing Juna as she remembered.

"Well, youngling, you may be on your way to becoming a Traegon Wayseer. Therefore, you shall have to look at things a bit differently now. I guess this is as good a time as any to begin your training," Oracle Balstar paused.

A Wayseer? Karia was caught off guard. She had not really thought of what all of this would mean. She had dreamed of this, but never really expected it to happen, at least not yet.

"Ravens are the guardians of the mystical thinkers or Wayseers." Oracle Balstar's voice broke into Karia's thoughts. "Each has one to assist them in different ways. One way is in travel. When a Wayseer travels alone, he travels upon his companion raven, and if he travels by another means, the raven is never far away: watching, guarding, protecting, and guiding."

Karia had rolled back over and was listening carefully as she watched the giant raven circling above.

"Is that your raven?" she asked dreamily.

"Yes, that is Sable. He has been with me for a very long time. He was just young when I became a Wayseer. I am afraid his head has become a bit inflated now that he is companion to the Oracle."

Karia continued to watch as Sable floated gracefully through the trees. "He is quite beautiful," Karia stated aloud.

"He will be proud to hear that," Oracle Balstar replied, and then they continued on in silence.

Karia thought more about the idea of becoming a Wayseer. It frightened her a little, but excited her a great deal. She wondered if she might have her own raven one day. Finally, they reached the willow tree. The Sentinel by the name of Nintar was waiting outside as they pulled up. He called a squire to take the bags and another to lead the wagon away. Oracle Balstar, Master Zoal, and Karia entered into the willow garden. Even though she had been there before, she was still in awe of its beauty. Oracle Balstar excused himself after asking Nintar to show Karia to her quarters. Karia followed Nintar back around the willow to where they had stayed before. Nintar opened the door and motioned Karia to enter. He followed after her.

"This is where you will be staying. If you are in need of anything, you may ring the chime outside your door and someone will come. Make yourself comfortable and I will return shortly to take you to Oracle Balstar. Rest for a while now and remember if you need anything, just ring your chime." Nintar turned and left.

Karia had never been on her own before. It seemed strange to her to be all alone in this place. The room was familiar, but quite large, at least for just one. She looked around and noticed her traveling bag was sitting on the bed. She walked over and thought about unpacking. She wondered how long she might be staying and felt lonely. She opened her bag and began to remove her belongings. Inside was a satchel of food that Mim had given her before she left. She sat in the large chair next to the bed and opened the satchel. Inside were all of her favorites: the berry and bug mix, a jar of sage tea, some of the walnut bread she had made for breakfast, and a cotton bag of sunflower seeds. Karia wasn't very hungry, but she nibbled on a little bit of the bread and that seemed to make her feel better.

She wrapped up the rest of the food and set it on the table for later. She was really missing her family now, and decided to lie down on the bed to rest.

A little while later, there was a soft knock on the door; when she opened it, she saw it was Nintar.

"Your presence is requested in Oracle Balstar's chambers. If you are ready, I will take you there now," he stated, with very little emotion.

"Yes, I am ready," answered Karia. She pulled the door closed behind her and followed Nintar through the garden and up the carved staircase to the room where she had first met Oracle Balstar.

Oracle Balstar stood as Karia entered. "Karia, come in and sit a while."

He motioned her to sit in one of two wooden chairs set off in a corner near a window. The setting sun lit the room with a warm, golden, afternoon glow.

"Your room is acceptable?" he questioned her as he sat in a chair opposite her.

"Yes, it is very nice," Karia answered.

"Excellent, it is important that you are comfortable," he continued. "As you know, I believe that this boy is the one that the prophecy speaks of. The previous evening, we brought him to your home through a process called Dream Walking. It is a way of summoning one to us without actually having them come on their own accord. If he were not the one, the likelihood of him coming and communicating with us would have been very slim. Now that we know that he can be summoned in this manner, we will attempt to bring him here, to the willow, in order that we may work with him as the prophecy states. Do you understand why you have come here to stay for a while?" he paused.

"I think I understand, but I do not understand why I had to leave my family. I miss them very much," Karia answered.

"Well, as I mentioned on our way here, you will be learning the ways of the Wayseers. Do you remember my speaking of this?" inquired Oracle Balstar.

"Yes, and I am honored."

"Well then, you must begin your training. You will work closely with me in bringing the boy here, and determining the exact role he is meant to play in this prophecy. There are many skeptics among our kind, who do not believe that this should be happening now. Therefore, we must be careful to ensure you follow the proper steps, which include learning the ways of the Wayseers. Do you understand, better now?" Oracle Balstar looked closely at Karia.

"Yes, I believe so," answered Karia.

"Good, now let us begin."

Chapter 11
Just a Dream

I didn't have any more experiences like the one I had the first night after receiving the white acorn, even though I continued to place it under my pillow each night before going to sleep, as Karia had instructed. This only confirmed to me that it had all been nothing more than a dream, and possibly just a product of my over-active imagination, and a little wishful daydreaming. I still couldn't explain how my journal got from under my mattress and into my jacket pocket, but I figured I must have been sleep-walking or something, and just put it there myself without remembering.

I spent as much of my after-school time as I could, drawing and writing in the journal, even though I first had to make time for my chores, homework, and occasionally hanging out with Quinn. I was looking forward to seeing Karia and Juna again this coming week-end, and worked to finish the picture I had started of Juna, as well as the one I had promised Karia in exchange for the acorn. It didn't even matter much if I couldn't keep the acorn. I was just glad that they liked my drawings and wanted to give them to them either way. Thinking about the dream I had, I felt an urge to draw a picture of Mim and Sire Argus, though I was worried that Mim and Sire Argus would look different than they did in the dream, and I feared that Karia and Juna wouldn't like the drawing. As I began to draw,

I began remembering more of my dream. Then I remembered what Karia had said, about it being all right if I wrote in the journal about the strange things that happened to me, to help me remember. So that is exactly what I did.

Chapter 12
Training Begins

B ack in Traegonia, Karia was in the process of learning the ways of the Wayseer. She would meet with Oracle Balstar in the garden each day following her morning meal. They would begin their session by sitting before to a giant crystal at the north end of the garden. Balstar had explained to Karia that each of the large crystals was placed in the garden in accordance with its significance to its specific directional power. The crystal placed in the north held the power of wisdom and guidance, and was charged each time it was thought upon. So that was how they began.

As Karia sat on one side of the crystal, Oracle Balstar situated himself across from her on the other side of the crystal. They would close their eyes and hold their hands up in front of them toward the crystal, but never directly touching it. The first time they did this, Karia was told to just sit and experience it. She was told not to think of anything specific, just to clear her mind and feel whatever might come.

The first thing she noticed was a warmth that seemed to be coming from the crystal, itself. Then a bright white light filled her mind. She tried to push it aside, thinking that she had created it, but it wouldn't go away. Finally, she just allowed it to be; enjoying the warmth that enveloped her. She felt the light pouring over her, from the top of her head down over her shoulders, moving over her entire being. She saw herself as if from outside of her body, watching as the light poured over her and onto the ground, creating a pool of light beneath her. She didn't feel frightened or alone; all she felt was warmth, safety, and complete comfort. Finally, the light completed its journey over Karia and the pool beneath her seeped into the earth. She sat quietly until she heard Oracle Balstar speak.

"You may open your eyes now, but just sit still for a few moments until you are completely grounded in this space."

Karia opened her eyes slowly and took a long deep breath. She felt that she wouldn't be able to move right away even if she wanted to, but she didn't want to. She was content to just sit as she was feeling very calm and very relaxed.

"That was wonderful, and very beautiful. Did you see the same thing that I saw?" she asked curiously.

"I am quite sure that what you saw is similar to what I saw, though all experience the charging differently," he answered in a soft slow voice.

"Charging?" Karia questioned. "What is charging?"

"Charging is when you bring yourself, or in your case are assisted, into a state of deep thought, and allow the purest energy to enter and cleanse you, and charge you with ethereal clarity," Balstar explained, as he stood and motioned for Karia to follow.

They walked slowly through the garden, listening to the songs of the chimes. As they approached the pool, Balstar held out his arm motioning Karia to sit. Karia looked into the pool of water and then back at Balstar.

"May I speak?" she asked.

Oracle Balstar sat at the pool and responded. "As you wish, say whatever comes to your mind."

"I really feel that Dino is the boy that the prophecy speaks of. I just have this feeling that he is somehow special. I do not fear him in the least. I actually trust him wholly. But I also do not wish to cause unease among our community," Karia said.

"Your instincts are innocent and pure, youngling. You now must begin to trust in yourself as much as you say that you trust in the boy. If I did not believe in your assumption, we would not be sitting here right now. Only once before had we thought the chosen child had come, but it was clear early on that she was not the one. I too have a good feeling about this child. Not all Traegons feel as Sir Dour feels. You mustn't feel that you are the only one who believes, but you must believe in yourself. Do you understand? No matter what happens, you must hold true to your convictions," Oracle Balstar concluded in a very convincing tone.

"Yes, Oracle, I understand," answered Karia.

"Now then, I want you to spend time in the garden. Walk around and look around. When you feel the time is right, go to the east end of the garden. Not far from the crystal there, you will find a willow basket containing your afternoon meal. Think, rest, and eat. When you are finished, proceed back to the North Crystal. There you will find a pile of stones. Spend some time there and then place the stones in a circle upon the ground. Place them as you feel they should be placed. Then you may return to your room. I will send Nintar to get you for our evening session."

Karia stared at Oracle Balstar as she took in all of his instructions. When he finished speaking, Karia nodded and Balstar stood and walked through a door that appeared in the trunk of the tree.

She was alone. It was completely quiet except for the chimes and the sound of the trickling water in the garden pool. A low growl came from deep inside her stomach. She stood and walked toward the east end of the garden, still feeling relaxed and calm. She found the basket and ate. The food was good, and very satisfying.

After eating, she proceeded to the pile of stones, back at the north end of the garden. Her first thought was that she was being tested, and that if she placed the stones incorrectly, she would fail the test. Thoughts of being tested overwhelmed her. She sat on the ground and stared at the stones. She closed her eyes and took a few deep breaths. When she opened her eyes, she knew exactly how she would place the stones. She created the circle, admired it for a moment or two, and then retired to her room.

Several hours later, Nintar knocked upon her door. "You are requested in the garden."

Karia followed him through the garden to the circle of stones, where Oracle Balstar was waiting. "The circle is perfect. Did it take you very long?" he asked.

"Not long," Karia responded.

"Tomorrow evening, you will summon the boy here and this circle will be your tool," stated Oracle Balstar, still staring at the stones.

"Me? I will summon him?" Karia asked curiously.

"Yes, you must be the one to call him here. I am able to bring in anyone, but if he comes when you summon him, well, that will be the result of the second test. The last time, the child did not come, and that was how we knew."

Karia felt a wave of fear as he told her about the previous results. But the fear passed quickly as she remembered to believe in herself and her conviction of who she believed Dino to be.

"How will I summon him?" she asked.

"We will begin by burning cedar in the center of the circle, and you will sit within the circle as well. You will close your eyes and silently call to him. You will visualize him in his world, and you will call to him. If it works as it should, he will appear in the circle with you, and if not, we will know the truth. If you wish, you may stay a while in the garden, or you may return to your room. It is your choice. But if you choose to stay, you must not attempt to contact him now, not even to practice. Do you understand?"

"I think I shall return to my room for sleep if that is all right," Karia responded.

"As you wish. Sleep well."

Karia and Balstar left the garden and retired for the night.

Chapter 13
Learning to Journey

Karia awoke very early the next morning. She hadn't slept well. She was excited about seeing Dino this night, but was also anxious about being able to summon him on her own. She sat quietly in her room thinking about how she would perform her summoning. What would she say? How would she be able to visualize his world if she had never seen where he lived? All of this was very overwhelming to her, and she hadn't spoken to Mim or Sire Argus in days, which didn't help with the way she was feeling.

Soon, there was a knock at her door. It was her morning meal, but this time when Karia opened the door, she saw it was not Nintar who brought it.

"It is expected to be a bright and beautiful day! Are you feeling well?" asked the Sentinel as she walked into the room. First, it was a she-Traegon, and second, she was much more cheerful than Nintar ever was.

"Who are you?" Karia asked inquisitively.

"A greeting would have been nice. But as you wish, I am Para. Oracle Balstar thought you might be more comfortable with a she Sentinel attending to your needs. I have brought your morning meal. When you are finished, Oracle Balstar wishes your presence in the garden. Do you know your way or would you like for me to return to escort you?" asked Para.

"I am very sorry. Good day to you, and many thanks for bringing this meal. I was just a bit surprised to see you and not Nintar. But it is very nice to meet you," Karia said, looking over the meal Para laid on the table. There seemed to be so much food and Karia was feeling a bit lonely. "I can find my way to the garden, but there is so much food here for just one, would you like to stay and share this meal with me?"

"How nice of you to ask, I would enjoy that very much. It will give us a chance to become more acquainted." Para sat down at the table and fixed Karia a plate and then one for herself. They ate and talked and ate and talked some more, Karia thoroughly enjoyed her company. When they finished, Para packed up the remainder of the food and dishes and together they headed for the door.

"Thank you for staying," said Karia, as they left the room.

Para smiled. "I will look in on you later." Para walked off toward the back of the tree and Karia proceeded on to the garden where Oracle Balstar was waiting.

"I am glad you are here, we have much to do in preparation of this eve. Did you meet Para?"

"Oh yes," Karia responded. "She is very kind and I greatly enjoyed her company. I am so grateful that you sent her."

"Excellent! Now let us begin. We will start in the north end of the garden," Balstar said, leading the way. "Following the charging, we will work on your summoning technique. I will not be able to completely prepare you for the experience, as all who attempt it find it quite different. But I will offer some guidance to assist you."

Karia took her place on one side of the crystal and Oracle Balstar on the other, and then they raised their hands toward the crystal and closed their eyes. The charging followed the same pattern as the day before, with the white light pouring over her and forming in a pool on the ground beneath her. Except this time, it didn't end there. Once the pool was on the ground, it stayed there. It began to sparkle with many colors, more colors than Karia even knew existed.

As the sparkles jumped and danced upon the pool of white light, she could feel a tingling sensation in her feet. The sparkling light grew around her, and the tingling was felt throughout her body. It wasn't exactly uncomfortable, just very different. Once the sparkling light completely surrounded her, it parted all at once like a curtain in front of her. There before her was a forest, but she knew that she was not really there. She felt herself take a step forward through the curtain. She looked around. It looked like the same forest where she had grown up, but at the same time it looked different. She couldn't place what was different about it, but it was beautiful nonetheless. She walked through the trees and was able to smell the clean crisp air and feel the breeze wisp past her face. All of a sudden, she had an overwhelming sense of danger. She quickly looked around but saw nothing. She couldn't identify her fear, nor could she explain it, but she was sure it was there, somewhere. She looked around for the sparkling curtain of light so that she could leave the forest, but it wasn't there. She closed her eyes and took a step backward. Suddenly, she felt herself being pulled back. She quickly opened her eyes and found herself back in front of the crystal, still seated. Karia leaned to look around the crystal for Oracle Balstar, but he was no longer there. She turned looking around the garden and saw him standing back away from the crystal, watching her.

"What happened?" Karia asked in a frightened tone.

"I do not know. I did not journey with you. Once the curtain opened and you stepped through, you were on your own. Come over here and sit. Tell me what it was that you saw on your journey," requested Oracle Balstar.

Karia stood but quickly sat back down. She felt dizzy and a little weak.

"Try again, only slower this time," he suggested. Karia took a deep breath and stood slowly. She turned and walked toward Oracle Balstar.

"Why do I feel so strange?" she asked.

"It is strenuous work what you just did. It takes time to adjust to these journeys."

"Journey? I thought that we were just charging?" Karia questioned.

"Charging is always and only the first step. Now, tell me what you experienced."

Karia sat on the ground across from Oracle Balstar. She began to feel much better. She placed her hands flat upon the earth and felt strength and stability. She could feel the warmth of the earth within her. She finally understood the meaning of being grounded.

"When the curtain opened, I found myself in the forest," Karia began. "I believe it was the same forest where I met Dino. It seemed strange, but also familiar. Then all of a sudden, I felt very frightened, but there was nothing there. Nothing at all, but I still felt this tremendous fear. Then I came back. What do you think scared me so?" Karia asked.

"I cannot be sure. There was nothing around you? No animals, no humans, nothing?" questioned Oracle Balstar.

"No, nothing, but even though I am back here, I still cannot release this feeling," observed Karia.

"Well, it is important that you allow yourself to feel this fear and honor your senses, but you must not allow the fear to keep you from continuing your work. This is important," Oracle Balstar said insistently. "Now we shall practice your preparation for the summoning. Just sit comfortably. You will only work within the circle when you are actually performing the summoning. Close your eyes and allow yourself to feel the earth beneath you. Listen only to the sound of your breathing, and the beating of your heart."

Karia did as she was told. She found herself beginning to become calmer and more relaxed. She began breathing deeply, and with each breath she relaxed further, her breathing becoming slower and melodic. She continued breathing and listening to the sound of her heartbeat. There came no more instruction. A long time passed before Oracle Balstar finally spoke again.

"Now, young one, take several deep breaths and slowly begin to open your eyes. Again, you will not want to move immediately."

Karia opened her eyes as instructed. She felt very heavy. She slowly stretched her arms and took several more deep breaths. "I feel a bit tired," she said slowly.

"That is perfectly normal, Karia. It will pass in a short while, and you will feel much better," Oracle Balstar assured her. "You will use this technique tonight when you call the boy. The circle is complete. You have experienced journeying, and learned the tools to summon. Now for the remainder of the day, you should think on these things and rest. I will send Para to retrieve you when the time comes. You are welcome to spend time in the garden if you wish. If you need to speak with me or are in need of anything else, just ring the chime outside your door and Para will come. Until tonight."

Oracle Balstar leaned on his crooked walking stick to help him stand, nodded, then turned and walked away.

Chapter 14
The Bad News

Over the next few days, I had completed the picture of Juna from our day in the woods, and was almost finished with the picture of Mim and Sire Argus, with as much detail as I was able to remember from my dream. I was greatly looking forward to seeing Karia and Juna this weekend, just a few more days. It had been raining all day and I was soaked by the time I got home from school. As I walked up the driveway, I noticed my dad's car in the driveway. He had gotten home before me today. I walked into the house and toward the kitchen where my parents were sitting, drinking tea, and talking quietly. When I stepped into the kitchen, they immediately stopped talking.

"Hi, Dad. Why are you home so early? You never beat me home."

"I had to go and survey some land for a new job that's coming up. I finished early and decided to call it a day. How was your day?" he asked, taking a sip of his tea.

Mom looked at me as Dad spoke, her look strangely solemn.

"Are you OK, Mom?" I asked.

"Yes, honey, I'm fine," she answered, not really convincing me that things were fine, but I figured if she wanted to tell me, she would.

"I've got some homework, I'm gonna go get started, OK?" I said, looking forward to finishing the pictures.

"Yes, that's fine, I'll call you when dinner is ready," Mom answered.

The evening was quiet, except for the occasional downpour and a crack of thunder here and there. After dinner, I returned to my room and spent the rest of the evening there. Mom and Dad talked a little more then sat quietly by themselves for the remainder of the evening.

When I finished my homework, I went downstairs to say goodnight to my parents. Dad was sitting at his desk working on some papers when I entered. The small desk lamp lit his face and I could tell that something was bothering him. He didn't notice me at first. "Dad? I just wanted to say goodnight," I hesitated. "Is there something wrong? Mom seems upset about something."

"Sit down, Dino," he said, looking up from his paperwork. "Your mom is upset. You know the survey I told you about today? Well, my company informed me that there is a development company that is looking a buying the land that borders the forest where we go on the weekends. This company wants to level the entire property and build a shopping mall. A large part of the forest is included in the land deal, and will disappear if the deal goes through."

My heart felt heavy and my stomach turned. I thought I was going to be sick. I swallowed hard.

"Dad that would be terrible, isn't there anything we can do to stop them? There are already lots of stores just up the street from the there. Why do they need more? Why do they need to mess up that place? It's beautiful there, and there are so many creatures that live there, where will they go?"

I felt and heard myself begin to panic. My dad stood and walked over to me. I grabbed his arm tight and looked straight into his eyes.

"Dad, we have to do something!"

"I love that place too, son. I'm not quite sure why you and your mother are so upset, but I trust her intuitions and I'm going to look into whether there is anything we can do. I have to get more information on the deal and who exactly holds the deed on the land currently. I am also going to call a friend of mine at the Forest Preserve tomorrow, and make sure they are aware that this land has gone up for sale. I don't know if there is anything more I can do, but I can promise you, as I did your mother, I will try. Now, Dino, go on to bed and try not to worry."

He leaned over and kissed the top of my head. I felt weak. He pulled me to my feet and sent me off to bed.

"Goodnight, Dino," I heard him say as I walked out of the room. I was feeling sick, so many thoughts raced through my mind that I couldn't even think straight.

I wandered into the room where my mom was. She was sitting on the couch reading a book.

"Mom?" I said in a quiet voice. "Dad told me why you are upset."

"Oh, Dino, I was hoping he would wait until we knew more. Honey, I honestly believe that there is a way to change this, I just don't know what that is right now. I promise you, we are all going to work together to try and save this forest," my mom said with determination in her voice. "I was sad when your father first told me, but now after I have thought about it more, I am just really angry. I'm not going to let some money-hungry corporation ruin this place for the sole purpose of making a few bucks. Not if I can help it."

Her words gave me hope. My mom is a strong woman, and when she got something in her head, she kept on it until she got what she wanted. If anyone could change this, I think she could.

"Thanks, Mom, I feel a little better now."

"Good, then you should go and get some sleep now. I may need your help tomorrow." She waved me over to where she was sitting and put her arms around me, hugging me really tight. "I love you, Dino. Goodnight and don't worry." She kissed my cheek and sent me off to bed.

"Goodnight, Mom." I turned and walked back to my room. I felt like I was in a fog. I lay down on my bed and tried to sleep. I tossed and turned, and then I remembered the acorn. I hadn't put it under my pillow. I reached under my bed and pulled out the wooden box, opened it, took out the acorn and held it for a moment, then finally placed it under my pillow. I fell asleep as soon as my head hit the pillow.

Chapter 15
The Summoning

Para brought Karia into the garden. It was dark except for the candle lanterns hanging throughout the garden, causing light to flicker and dance off of the crystals. Oracle Balstar was waiting by the stone circle, but this time he wasn't alone. Master Zoal and the other elders were seated on larger stones set back away from the circle. Karia wasn't expecting an audience. She walked up to Oracle Balstar.

"Why is everyone here?" she asked politely.

"They must be witnesses to the summoning. If he comes tonight, we will have many questions for him and much to tell him. Do not worry, all who are here believe in this work, and in your ability," Oracle Balstar assured her. "Now, enter the circle and make yourself comfortable."

Karia entered the circle. She tried to block out the knowledge that there were so many eyes upon her. She sat down, using a small white candle that stood in a handled holder, she lit the few cedar sprigs that lay in the bottom of an abalone shell. She watched as the flame flared and then quickly burned out, leaving the glowing, smoldering cedar. The smoke rose up out of the bowl and began to encircle her. She closed her eyes and listened to the beating of her heart. BA-bum, ba-bum, ba-bum. She breathed deeply and listened again. BA-bum, ba-bum, ba-bum. In her mind she saw the white light begin to sparkle above her head, silently she called to it; she called to it for guidance and protection. She breathed in the light and allowed it to pour over her and let the warm energy comfort her. Through the light, she could still hear the beating of her heart.

She began to imagine what Dino's room might look like. She pictured it as clearly as possible in her thoughts. With every beat of her heart, she could feel herself being pulled, pulled backward, BAbum, ba-bum, and suddenly she fell.

Finally, she stopped tumbling and felt herself land softly. She slowly opened her eyes. There she was, lying in a pile of clothes on the floor of Dino's bedroom. Karia looked around and noticed Dino's bed across the room, with him lying asleep on top. She quietly walked over to the bed and climbed up the foot board. She moved slowly and silently up to where he lay sleeping.

"Dino, Dino wake up," Karia whispered. She placed her hand on his cheek and pushed as hard as she could. "Dino, Dino, wake up now!"

—————•((●))•—————

As I rolled over, I heard a thud. I sat up quickly and looked around.

"Hey, Dino!" a whispered voice called up from the floor. "Help me up!" I leaned over and looked down at the floor beside my bed, and there was Karia pulling on the blanket in an attempt to climb up the side.

"Hold on tight," I said and I pulled the blanket up along with Karia. "What are you doing here?" I asked her.

"You have to come with me. Get the acorn," answered Karia in a hurried voice.

"But I'm not dressed," I told her, looking down and realizing that not only was I dressed, but I already had my jacket on. I grabbed the acorn from under my pillow and followed Karia across the room.

"Sit on the floor here," she directed.

"What's going on?" I asked as I sat down where she told me to.

"All of your questions will be answered soon. Now please just do as I tell you," Karia responded. She seemed slightly preoccupied and very serious.

"Now I will stand here beside you. Hold the acorn in your left hand and my hand in your right. Close your eyes and whatever you do, don't let go."

We both closed our eyes. Moments later, I felt as if I was being pulled backward. Immediately, we were both transported safely into a circle in a garden. We opened our eyes and looked at each other. Again, Karia and I were the same size. I looked around at this amazing place she brought me to.

"How did you do that? Where are we?" I began to blast her with questions.

When I looked back at her, she was standing facing me, but looking past me. I stood up and turned to see what she was looking at. There standing before us were eight Traegons, two of whom I had seen before in my last dream. I didn't recognize the others, and Karia's family wasn't there, nor was Juna. I glanced back at Karia.

"What's going on?" I asked her.

Oracle Balstar answered my question for her. "Dino, it is good to see you again. Welcome to Traegonia. Karia, young one, you have accomplished something I only wished to see happen in my lifetime. You are on your way to greatness among the Traegon community."

I think that we were both overwhelmed with what he had said. I looked over at Karia, who was now standing next to me with her mouth hanging open. I put my hand under her long chin and pushed her mouth closed. "You're gonna let the bugs in," I said jokingly. She looked at me with wide eyes and smiled.

"Come now, both of you, let us sit and speak of these things that have happened," Oracle Balstar broke in.

A table had been set in the garden filled with food and drink. All of the Traegon elders were staring at me as we walked to the table to sit. Once we were seated, Oracle Balstar introduced the elder council members, and instructed Karia to tell me everything. Karia explained everything from as far back as the first time we had met to now, and finished by telling me that I was the chosen one, the one their prophecy had spoken of. I couldn't speak. My mouth and throat were very dry. I was still wondering if this was all a dream. Suddenly, I felt Karia push my mouth closed.

"You're gonna let the bugs in," she said, smiling.

I took a sip of tea from the wooden cup sitting on the table in front of me and asked, "Is this a dream? I feel like I am waiting to wake up."

"No, this is definitely not a dream. You, Dino, are the first human to enter into our world, by way of a Traegon youngling," answered Sir Gortho. "We are honored by your presence and welcome you."

I sat quietly for a few moments, trying to sort through all of this in my mind. Suddenly, I remembered what my father had told me before I went to bed.

"Where is this place, Traegonia?"

"There are many Traegonias," a soft voice spoke, "this one though, lies deep in this forest. It is not far from the place where you and Karia met, and where her family lives. This forest, this land encompasses our whole village, our entire world is here," answered Madam Calthia.

"I think I may know why I am here," I said solemnly.

"What is it, Dino?" Karia asked, looking at me with deep concern on her face.

"I just found out, my father told me earlier this evening," I began.

"What is it? What do you know?" Karia broke in before I could finish.

"Let the boy speak, Karia," Oracle Balstar scolded gently.

"Some people are trying to buy this land. They are planning to tear down the forest to build a shopping mall," I exclaimed.

"What is a shopping mall?" Karia asked.

A tall regal looking male Traegon stood and removed the pipe from his mouth. "A needless structure made of brick and metal that will probably only have use for a short time and then will stand empty and neglected," piped in Sir Antar.

"In many ways, this is true," I confirmed. "It is meant to hold stores where people can go to buy things that they need."

"Things that humans need? How much of what is in these places are really needs? I do believe that more of these things are wants, not needs," retorted Sir Antar.

"We are not here to debate the realistic necessity of these buildings to humans. We are here to ensure the existence of Traegonia, and that all Traegons' are not decimated," Oracle Balstar broke in.

Karia turned to Sir Antar. "How do you know so much about the human world?"

"I have had the rare opportunity to see some of these things." He paced behind the table. "I work with a group in the village known as the Unpuzzliers. Their work is to find solutions to problems and situations the community is faced with. We have many times had to research human existence, and we have tried, without avail I might add, to figure out the reasons for some of their actions. Though we have never been faced with anything of this magnitude," responded Sir Antar.

"This is a very serious and frightening situation. We must work together to quickly find a solution," Madam Calthia said. "Dino, do you know how soon all of this will be transpiring?"

"Please know that my family and I are all very upset about this situation. My family will try everything they can to stop this from happening," I tried to offer some hope.

"How soon?" Karia repeated Madam Calthia's question.

"I don't know." I looked down, feeling helpless.

"And why, may I ask, would your family care what happens to this forest?" asked Madam Taendia.

"My mom and dad both enjoy coming to this forest and also believe that there isn't a need for any more shopping malls. They love nature and wish for more people to care enough about the Earth to take better care of it. We believe that it is important to keep as much of the land as possible the way it is and has been from the beginning, for the animals and other creatures," I responded, feeling protective of my parents. "My family and I are not like the humans you have seen and there are others like us, as well. Please don't treat us like the enemy. We want to help."

"We know that you are different, Dino, otherwise you would not be here. I did not mean to dishonor you or your family. Please forgive us if we have caused you to feel defensive." Madam Calthia tried to calm me.

"First, we will need to explore to what extent the humans have begun their process of eliminating these lands. I believe the Unpuzzliers would be best suited to begin an investigation from above to determine what if anything has already begun." Sir Gortho began to lay the plan. "We must first find out if they have acquired the land yet. If they have not, it may be necessary to pay a visit to the elderly couple who live upon this land as well."

"Yes, Gortho, I believe that may be an unprecedented but necessary strategy," replied Oracle Balstar.

"I am actually quite surprised that the elderly couple has even agreed to relinquish their land to such humans. I have known of these humans since I was young. They were always very kind to the creatures of the forest, and to us," added Madam Shoran. "This couple has occupied that land for as long as I can remember. When they built their home there, they were very careful not to remove more of the natural surroundings than was absolutely necessary."

She looked at Madam Calthia, who nodded a silent approval.

Madam Shoran continued explaining, "I have never told anyone this before, but now seems to be a good time to share. As young Traegons, Madam Calthia and I would go there and watch them. We had heard of them and just had to see for ourselves. The woman always fed the forest creatures, and the man would build shelters for any homeless creature who wished to dwell there. I have seen them, with my own eyes, care for creatures who were broken and orphaned. They never harmed a one, only helped. I remember once when food was scarce and it was colder than ever before, they laid out so much food that even my Sire went there in order that we would not go hungry. I believe that many Traegon families have paid visit to them in times past."

"Yes, I must agree. That is exactly what happened to my family as well during that same terrible cold," Madam Calthia added. "I too will share with you something I have never shared with another, even you, Shoran."

We all watched intently, curious as to what she would say. Madam Calthia continued. "Once when I was very young, following that terrible cold, I, too, had gone to see these kind and generous humans. I wanted to thank them somehow, but did not know how. It was during the time of the budding trees and the air was warm. The woman was making food and the windows of their home were open. She placed this wonderfully sweet smelling circular dish upon the windowsill. The scent mesmerized me. I just had to have a small taste. I slowly made my way from the safety of the forest to just below the open window. I carefully climbed to the sill and was preparing to take a small piece when I looked up and saw the woman staring at me. In my fright, I slipped off of the sill, taking the food down with me. I jumped up and ran as fast as I could back to the forest. I could tell by the look upon her face that she was as surprised to see me as I was to see her.

"I waited in the forest for a few moments trying to catch my breath when I heard the door open. I closed my eyes tight so as not to be discovered, until I heard the door open and close again. I looked out to see if she had gone, when I noticed that she had brought the food almost to the edge of the forest. She was giving it to me. I looked back at the house and could see her in the window. 'Enjoy your pie, dear, and come back any time,' "She called to me. And I did so enjoy the pie, as she called it." Madam Calthia closed her eyes and breathed deeply as if smelling the pie again.

"I left the rest for the other creatures nearby. After that, I was never afraid to go there and I went often. I never let her see me again though. I knew better, but I think she knew when I was around."

We all stared at Madam Calthia in amazement as she finished her story. I guess she was now too grown up to get in trouble for this.

"All Traegons know of these humans, and I too am surprised they have chosen to turn over this land to those who wish to harm it," responded Master Zoal, looking up from his writing.

"I guess it is becoming clear why the time is now that the prophecy should come to pass. We have much work to do. Dino, your assistance will be needed. You must find out all that you can about this situation from your world. Sir Antar, set a meeting with the Unpuzzliers to lay out your course of action. Madam Calthia and Madam Shoran, I would like the both of you to accompany Arbalest and Karia to the home of the elderly couple. See what you can find out, without making contact with them. We will later determine if and when we may need to visit them directly. Sir Gortho, Madam Taendia, and Master Zoal, I wish for you three to track the efforts of the groups, and work on strategies if in fact we do have to vacate our village. Do we all understand our duties?" asked Oracle Balstar.

Everyone looked around at each other and nodded that they understood.

"Dino, you must return home for now. Do you believe that you will be able to perform your tasks?" Oracle Balstar looked at me in a serious way.

"Yes, sir, I will do everything I can to help. When will I see you again?" I asked.

"Karia and Juna will meet you in your usual place in the forest as planned. You will return here in time as is necessary, once we begin to obtain more information," Oracle Balstar assured me.

I looked over at Karia and she had a look of delight on her face. I think that she was excited about going back to the forest this weekend. I was too.

Oracle Balstar stood to address us. "Master Zoal, I would like for you to put the word out to the community that the prophecy is coming to fruition; that the boy is the one the prophecy spoke of, and that Karia and Juna have done a great service for our village. Do not offer any indication to the community, though, of the pending nature of our work. We must keep things quiet for now to ensure panic is not generated throughout the community. Karia, it is now time for you to take Dino home."

Karia stood and motioned for me to follow. I stood and spoke to the group. "Thank you for inviting me here. It was very nice to meet you all and I will do my very best for you."

I followed Karia to the circle of stones and sat down beside her. She instructed me to close my eyes and hold onto her hand. I did as she asked.

Chapter 16
What to Do?

I woke up to my mom's voice calling to me to get up for school. There was a bit of irritation in her voice and I wondered if she had been calling me for long.

"I'm up, Mom, I'll be down in a few minutes," I called back to her.

As I dressed for school, I began to recall my dream about seeing Karia and the others in the garden. I started to think that it might be more real than I had originally thought. I reached under my pillow to put away the acorn and it was gone. I threw my pillow on the floor and tore back my bedcovers, nothing. I stopped and turned around, looking at my jacket. As I walked toward it, I thought to myself, *if the acorn is in my pocket, then my dream must have been real.*

I pushed my hand deep into the pocket of my jacket and felt around. It was there, along with my pencil and my journal. I removed the acorn and my journal. I put the acorn away in the box under my bed and sat down to write what I could remember of my dream. Moments later, my mom was calling for me to hurry and come down for breakfast.

"Your breakfast is going to get cold, and you're going to be late for school if you don't come down here right now," she hollered.

The tone of her voice seemed strange to me. I grabbed my jacket and raced down the stairs, shoving my journal into my pocket. When I reached the kitchen, I could see that my mother was frenzied. She looked up at me and began moving large pieces of cardboard, wooden sticks, markers, and paint off to one side of the table, making room for me to sit and eat my breakfast. She placed a bowl of cereal and some toast in front of me, poured herself another cup of coffee, and sat down at the table with me. I looked at her over the stacks of materials piled on the table, and could tell that she had other things on her mind.

"Where's Dad?" I asked.

"He left for work early this morning. Do you have all of your things ready for school?" she answered me and asked her question all in the same breath.

"All except for my lunch," I said, taking a bite of my toast. She looked at the clock and leaped from her chair. "Shoot, I forgot to make it. I'll have it ready in just a minute." Frantically, she grabbed the bread and lunch meat from the refrigerator and dropped it on the counter.

"I can buy my lunch today if you want, Mom," I said, hoping to calm her down. She leaned over the counter and put her head in her hands.

"Are you all right, Mom?" I asked.

"I think buying your lunch would be a good idea," she answered.

"Mom, what's wrong?" I asked again.

"Oh, Dino, I didn't get much sleep last night. I have just been thinking about that land and the developer who wants to buy it. I just hope we're not already too late."

"Is that what all this stuff is for?" I asked.

"Yes, I am going to make signs and put them up all along the road near the forest. I think we need to let people know what's happening. I think a lot of people would agree that this land shouldn't be turned into a shopping mall. At least I hope they do." She sat back down at the table.

"It's going to be okay, Mom, please try not to get so upset. I really think everything will be alright. Dad won't let them do this," I told her, trying to help her feel better, still not understanding completely why she was so upset. "Quinn and I will go with you after school to help put the signs up."

She took a deep breath, looked at me, and smiled. "Thank you, I will make as many as I can while you're at school."

She took some money from a jar in the cupboard and handed it to me.

"This is for your lunch. You'd better get going so you're not late." She kissed me on the forehead and I got up, grabbed my book bag, and left for school.

At school, all I could think about was my dream, and how everything that was happening was fitting together. I was also worried about what would happen if we couldn't stop them from building the mall. *What would happen to the Traegons?* I wondered where they would go.

Quinn and I went straight to my house after school. My mom was sitting at the kitchen table having a cup of tea. As soon as we walked in, I could tell that her mood was a lot better than it had been this morning.

"Hi, Mom! We're home! Ready to get started?"

"Hi, Dino! Hi, Quinn! Did you both have a good day at school?" she asked, very calmly.

"Yeah, school was good," answered Quinn. "Have you got anything to eat, Mrs. Dosek?"

"Yeah, it was okay, same old stuff, anything new with you?" I asked, actually meaning if there was anything new with the forest.

"No, I haven't heard anything about the land sale yet," she said, digging through the pantry and pulling out some cookies for Quinn and me. "I finished the signs and have them in the car. If you two don't have too much homework, maybe we can run these over first."

"Let's go," I said. "We can do our homework when we get back."

Quinn grabbed a handful of cookies and we got in the car and drove to the forest. There were a lot of people hanging around the forest, a lot more than usual. We pulled in where we always went for our picnics. Mom parked the car and we got out. We went around to the trunk and pulled out the signs. As we walked toward the street, we were approached by a tall thin man in a dark suit. Mom started to pound one of the signs into the ground when the man walked up and spoke to us.

"Do you have permission to put these signs up?" he asked in a low growl of a voice.

"And who may I ask are you?" said my mom, as she stood back up.

"I am Roger Billson, owner of Billson Developers. I can see that you are not too excited about the prospect of the coming mall."

"No, we're not happy about it at all. As a matter of fact, we think there are enough stores, and empty ones at that. Wouldn't it make more sense to use a building that is already built and standing empty?" responded my mother.

"Well, Miss, I am going to allow my attorneys to address all of the questions to the people in this and the surrounding communities, so you will have to contact them. But, I will tell you this, you're not likely going to make much of a difference with your little signs, and you do need permission. So why don't you take your signs and go home," Mr. Billson stated in a very condescending manner.

My mom took a step forward and looked him straight in the eye. "Thank you for the information, Mr. Billson, but I do believe you forgot to give me your attorney's name and number, and by the way, I do believe that I just might be able to make a difference, and I will be back with the proper permission."

Mr. Billson handed her a business card with the attorney's name and phone number on it. "Don't underestimate me, sir! Good day!" She pulled up the sign and turned to walk away, with Quinn and me following.

"I didn't catch your name?" the man called from behind us.

"That is because I didn't give it to you," answered my mother, without even turning around.

When we got back home, my mom thanked Quinn for offering to help, and gave him some extra cookies to take home. I went to my room to do my homework while she started dinner. I heard her pick up the phone as I walked up the stairs. I sat down at my desk and pulled my homework out of my book bag. When I looked at my assignment book, I realized that tomorrow was Friday, and we would be going to the forest in just two days. I had almost forgotten with all that was going on. It really seemed like it had been a very long week. I was excited about seeing Karia and Juna again, and telling them about my dreams, and of course, giving them the pictures I had promised. I finished my homework and was just putting my books away when I heard my father come home. I quietly walked to the top of the stairs to listen.

"Hi, honey!" my dad said, as he kissed my mom on the cheek.

"Hi! How was your day, Jack?" asked my Mom.

"Long. How was yours?"

"Well, I had the pleasure of meeting the developer who wants to purchase the land," Mom said sarcastically. She went on to tell him what had happened when we tried to put up the signs. That's when I decided to go on downstairs.

"Hi, Dino! How was school?" Dad asked as I entered the room.

"It was fine," I answered, sitting at the table.

"So when I called the Forestry Department, I was told that I couldn't put my signs up on their property because they didn't want any trouble with the developers," Mom continued.

"Yes, I know," Dad said, pulling up a chair. "Here, sit down." He motioned for my mom to sit at the table. "I spoke with my friend Charlie down there this morning. I guess they received a call from the developer asking them not to take sides on the issue."

"Not to take sides? How could the Forestry Department not care if the land bordering their preserve is destroyed? Don't they care? Aren't they in the business of preservation of land?" Mom was getting more and more upset.

"Calm down. I even went as far as to ask him if there was any way that the Forestry Department might be able to intercept the land sale and buy it themselves," my dad continued. "He told me that the only way they would be able to get funding for that land was if it was deemed protected."

"What does that mean?" I asked.

"Well, if there were some reason that the land should be preserved," Dad explained. "Like some of the old buildings in town. They have historical significance, so the government gives the owners special money to maintain it and keep it the way it originally was. Do you understand?"

"Yeah, I think so. Like if there was some tree or plant or animal or something that was endangered and needed protecting. Right?" I answered.

"That's right. Then they might step in and do something," Dad said.

"Well, that's good, isn't it, Jack? There has to be something out there." Mom's voice sprang with excitement.

"Well, hold on, Anna." Dad put his hand up. "There are almost thirty acres in question here, much of which is densely wooded. They just don't have the manpower to search all of that land. It would be like trying to find a needle in a haystack. Besides, you have to have someone who knows what is protected. I'm sure there are tons of things from this area that we have never even seen before."

"Well, aren't we even going to try? What are they going to do, just stand by and watch the land get leveled?" Mom said, anger growing in her voice.

"He is still going to talk to some other people in the department and see if anything can be done. He did mention starting a petition." Dad looked at Mom.

"Fine, Jack, I will start that tomorrow. All of this bureaucracy is ridiculous," Mom declared, as she pushed herself away from the table. "Let's eat before dinner gets cold."

We ate dinner in silence and when I was finished, I asked to be excused to my room.

"We are going to the forest this weekend, right?" I asked, walking toward the stairs. They looked at each other.

"It would probably be a good idea if for no other reason than to get our minds off of things for a few hours," Mom suggested.

"Yeah, who knows, I just might catch an endangered blue gill or something," Dad said with a chuckle.

I was relieved and excited. I went to bed early that night looking forward to seeing Karia and Juna soon.

Chapter 17
Uncovering Why

Karia was called upon very early the next morning, to meet in the garden as soon as possible. She entered the garden and was met by Oracle Balstar, Arbalest Bendbow, Madam Calthia, and Madam Shoran.

"You must get an early start, as it is quite a distance to where the elderly couple live," stated Oracle Balstar as Karia walked up to the group. "You must be careful not to be discovered. It is possible that there will be others nearby. Go and ascertain what you can and return with your findings." Oracle Balstar turned and disappeared into the back of the garden.

The group exited the garden to a rabbit-drawn wagon waiting just outside the willow. Arbalest helped Madam's Calthia and Shoran onto the wagon, and then assisted Karia into the back. As they headed off into the darkness, Karia thought about the next day when she would meet Dino and Juna in the forest. She had not seen her family in what seemed like a very long time, and she missed Juna very much. The sun began to peek over the horizon and Karia sat up in the back of the wagon, and asked, "Are we near yet?"

Arbalest laughed. "Do you ask Sire Argus and Mim that same question when you journey with them?"

Karia thought for a moment and laughed at herself. "I see,

Arbalest. Yes I do, and usually much too often for Sire Argus' liking."

"We will be approaching the edge of the forest soon enough," Arbalest informed her.

Off in the distance, they could see a break in the forest wall. Madam Shoran reached over and grasped Madam Calthia's arm. "We are almost there. It has been a long time. My heart is pounding so."

"Yes, Shoran, I feel much the same way. It is almost like coming home," sighed Madam Calthia.

Arbalest pulled the wagon under a large fir tree and assisted the Madams' out. Karia jumped out of the wagon before Arbalest had a chance to help her. She ran to the edge of the forest and peered out from behind a large thistle bush. She saw a pretty little white house sitting in a large clearing, surrounded on all sides by forest.

"Is that it?" Karia asked her excitement mounting.

"Yes, my dear youngling, that is the place," answered Madam Calthia. "It seems so quiet. I expect that they may still be asleep. Karia, you and Arbalest should go up to the home and see what you can. The two of you are younger and can move much faster than we can, should someone come. We will wait here for you."

Arbalest swung his bow over his shoulder and squatted down beside the thistle bush at the edge of the forest. He motioned to Karia to move in close behind him. He surveyed the area to see if there was anyone about, all was quiet, almost too quiet. "Keep silent and follow close to me," he directed Karia. "I will motion to you as needed, and if perchance we should be in danger of being detected, run as fast as you can back into the tree line and take cover under the fir tree. Understood?"

Karia nodded.

They began to slowly move out of the protective cover of the thistle bush, staying very aware of any noises or movement. They ran from tree to bush and to another tree, as they made their way to the house. Arbalest directed Karia to wait by a tree closest to the house while he went to the rear porch steps. He whispered for her to watch for his signal when all was clear, and then she should come on. When Arbalest reached the back porch, he noticed an empty rusty pan sitting on the bottom step and the bird feeder nearby was also empty. Arbalest spotted a hanging pot near an open window and decided that would be their way in. He motioned to Karia for her to come over now, and she moved quickly to the porch. Arbalest pointed to the hanging pot and patted his bow. He pulled his bow from over his shoulder and loaded it. He took aim and an arrow shot from his bow and wrapped itself around one of the chains that the pot was hanging from. Arbalest tugged hard on the rope, still attached to the arrow, and directed Karia to begin the ascent to the window. Karia looked at the rope and then at Arbalest with concern in her eyes.

"I don't know if I can do this," she whispered, "and what should I do when I reach the top?"

"Karia, you can do this," Arbalest assured her. "I will be holding the rope until you are in, and then I will follow. When you get to the pot, look in the window and make sure that no one is around. Then I will swing the pot close to the window so that you can grab onto the sill. Then you climb in and find a place to hide until I am able to get inside with you. Just stay out of sight."

Karia reluctantly took hold of the rope and slowly began to climb. The pot started to swing and Arbalest pulled tight on the rope to keep it steady. Karia looked down at Arbalest, and he nodded for her to continue on. As Karia reached the pot, she grabbed onto the edge and pulled herself up. The flowers, that once bloomed there, were now dried and crunchy. Karia sat in the pot and peered into the window. She could see no one, but she could hear soft music and voices coming from another room. She motioned to Arbalest that it was clear, and he began to swing the pot from side to side. As Karia came close to the window, she reached out and grabbed the sill. Her hand slipped and the pot swung back. She heard a noise from above her and looked up. The hook at the top of the chain was beginning to straighten out. Karia looked down at Arbalest, distressed.

Arbalest swung the pot again and this time, he moved with the rope, pulling it toward the window with all of his strength. "NOW!" he urged in a low whisper. Karia jumped to the windowsill and found herself hanging more out than in. She pulled with all of her strength, her legs kicking, and finally managed to pull herself up onto the sill. She was taking another look around when all of a sudden, she heard a huge thud from behind her. The noise startled her and she fell through the window and landed upon a large soft chair. When she looked up, she saw that the pot was no longer hanging outside the window; it had fallen. Karia heard movement in the next room. Someone was coming! She jumped over the arm of the chair and took cover behind it. Footsteps creaked across the floor. She could hear them coming closer. She held her breath, closed her eyes and leaned hard into the back of the chair. A man walked up next to the chair and looked out the open window. He noticed the pot lying on the ground beneath the window. Karia watched as he sighed and rubbed his eyes, then he turned and walked slowly out of the room.

Karia released her breath. She wondered if Arbalest was OK, and how he would get inside now. She also wondered how she would get out. She waited for a little while when she heard the back door open. That was her chance! She came out from behind the chair and looked around the room. It was dark, only a small amount of light streaming through the window. She moved slowly across the room, making sure to be aware of where her next hiding place would be if the man came back. She wondered where the kind old woman she had heard about was. Karia was looking forward to seeing her, and had hoped that she might have one of those pies for her to try. But there was nothing cooking on this day.

Dino C. Crisanti

Karia and Arbalest

Karia reached the door leading into the next room. There was a large table with chairs all pushed in, except for one. She could see a tea cup and a plate sitting at the edge of the table. The voices and music she heard were coming from a box on the counter. Suddenly, she heard footsteps coming back toward the room. Karia scrambled to hide under the table, which wasn't much of a hiding place. She noticed a jacket hanging from the back of one of the chairs. *That would be a better place to hide,* she thought. Karia sat down under the chair and was well hidden by the coat. The man came back into the room and sat down in the chair next to her. Moments later, she could hear the man weeping. She felt sad for him. He leaned forward and laid his head in his arms, still weeping.

Two pieces of paper floated to the floor, near where Karia was sitting. One of the pieces of paper had a picture of flowers and some writing on it. The other paper was face down on the floor, and when Karia turned it over, it was a picture of the man and the elderly woman. Karia suddenly felt a heaviness in her belly. She knew at that moment why the man wept. She remembered the way the tiny squirrel had wept after his family was killed in the storm. Karia stared at the picture and knew that the old woman was no longer in the house. That explained the empty pan and bird feeder, the dried up flowers, and no pies cooking, and now she had the answer to why the land was being sold.

Karia could feel the cold sadness that permeated the once warm and happy home. The man sniffled and took a drink from his cup. Then he stood and walked into the other room.

This was Karia's chance to get out. She crawled to the back of the chair and lifted the bottom of the jacket to make sure that no one was in the room. She had no idea which way she should go to get out of the house. She looked around. The room she had come out of was on one side. The man had just walked through another doorway directly in front of her, which left only one other possible option; the opening next to her. Karia stayed under the table until she got as close as possible to where she was going to go out. Then she took a deep breath, one last look, and darted for the doorway. As she turned the corner, she ran right into Arbalest. She bumped into him hard and fell backward to the floor.

"Arbalest!" Karia whispered, her heart pounding. "I know why they are selling the land."

"We have to get out of here, now." Arbalest helped Karia to her feet. "This way!" He grabbed her arm and pulled her in the direction of the door.

Finally outside, Karia noticed the once-hanging flowerpot now sitting on a table next to the door, and a pile of dirt with old dried flowers poking through, on the ground beneath where the pot once hung. "I am glad you are all right, Arbalest. I was concerned for your safety," Karia said, looking back from the pot.

"I too am glad that you are safe," he responded. "Now let us return to the wagon."

Arbalest and Karia made their way back to the wagon where Madam Shoran and Madam Calthia were waiting. As they reached the edge of the forest, they heard a loud grumbling sound. Karia peeked through the brush and saw a giant vehicle moving up the gravel path to the home. Arbalest touched her on the shoulder.

"It is time to go Karia," he said.

"Arbalest, look at that. What kind of wagon is it, with nothing to pull it?" Karia asked in amazement.

"It is what the humans use to move around long distances. It is best to stay away from them. The humans can't see anything below their noses when they are in them, and just run over everything." Arbalest tried to answer her question the best he could. "Now let us get going. We have a long way to travel before dark." They quickly climbed into the wagon and began their trek back to Traegonia.

The car pulled up to the house. Mr. Billson and another man stepped out and approached the front door. They knocked hard. The old man opened the door slowly. He peeked out, his eyes red and drawn.

"Mr. Rhodes! Good day. I just wanted to stop by and see if you are ready to sign these papers. I have them all drawn up for you," Mr. Billson said, with a big smile on his face.

Mr. Rhodes looked at Mr. Billson. "It is too early. Why didn't you call before you came over? I could have saved you the trip." Mr. Rhodes growled. "I told you I would need to think things over. I just buried my wife yesterday. I told you this, two days ago when you first came here."

"Well, sir, I am just trying to help you out. The sooner you are out of this house and not having to face the memory of your wife anymore, the better," Mr. Billson said, still in his upbeat tone.

"I would like to hold onto her memory if you don't mind. I will consider your offer when I am ready. If that isn't putting you out," Mr. Rhodes said sarcastically.

"Well, I suppose I could give it a few more days, but the clock is a-tickin' and we want to start clearing this debris as soon as possible. You know, before this old shack falls down around you. We're just looking out for your best interest here," chuckled Mr. Billson.

Mr. Rhodes sighed. "I need more than a few days."

"Oh, you drive a hard bargain. Hold on to these papers. Look them over and give me a call. I will come and get them. No need to pay anyone to look them over, we are really working for you, Mr. Rhodes. We just want to help out a friend in a bind. I'll call you in a week." Billson handed the envelope to Mr. Rhodes through the crack in the door.

"Two weeks or don't bother coming back." Mr. Rhodes slammed the door.

Mr. Billson turned to the other man who was with him. "He sure is a grumpy old man. I can't wait till we're through with him. Let's go drive around the land and go over the site plans."

Chapter 18
Devising a Plan

It was finally the weekend, and I was more excited than ever to be going to the forest. Definitely more excited than my mom and dad. They were still feeling worried about the land sale. With all that had gone on this past week, I had so much to talk to Karia and Juna about. I got up very early and got dressed. I made sure that I had the acorn and my journal before leaving my room. We ate a quiet breakfast, and then headed out for the day. Mom and Dad didn't have much to say. As soon as we reached the forest and unloaded the car, I asked if I could go off into the woods. They said I could go, but asked me to be extra careful today. They said that there may be more people around than usual. I knew that they were referring to Mr. Billson and others like him. As I walked deeper into the woods, I began to call for Karia and Juna. I tried to call quietly, which is a tough thing to do. Juna was the first to pop out from behind a clump of trees.

"Is Karia not here yet?" Juna asked, sounding sort of disappointed.

"No, I thought she would be with you," I responded.

Juna looked at the ground. "I have not seen her in many days," he said sadly.

I was just about to say something to try and comfort him when

Karia burst through the brush. "Juna!" Karia's voice bounded with excitement and relief.

Juna spun around and ran right into Karia's arms. They hugged for a long time. "Karia, I am so glad to see you. I have missed you terribly!" Juna said, as he stepped back.

"I too have missed you, Juna. I have been waiting so long for this day to come," responded Karia. I stood watching their reunion until they both turned and looked at me. I must have looked like I felt left out or something, because in unison, they said, "And we missed you too, Dino."

We all laughed and sat down under a very tall cedar tree. I pulled out my journal and carefully tore out the picture of Juna and handed it to him. The look on his face was one of complete amazement. Karia looked over his shoulder and smiled.

"Do you like it?" I asked.

Juna looked up and nodded his head. "Oh yes, it is very, very good. You really are magic."

I laughed as I looked over at Karia. She seemed to have a quiet joy in her eyes.

"I have another picture I would like to show you." I turned to another page and laid my journal upon the ground in front of them. They both looked silently at the book. It was a picture of Mim and Sire Argus from the first night I had visited Karia and Juna's home. Karia reached out and touched the page, then looked up at me with a pleading look on her face.

"Dino, may I have this picture? I have not seen them since that night," she stated. I could feel her sadness, and knew how I would feel if I was taken away from my family, even if it was for a really good reason. I wanted so much to help her to feel better and if the picture would help, then of course she could have it.

"It's yours," I said, ripping the page out of my journal and handing it to her.

Dino C. Crisanti

Juna

"I have no words to tell you how grateful I am. Your generosity fills my heart. Thank you," Karia said, bowing her head as she took the picture.

I was so happy that Karia and Juna liked the pictures I had drawn. We talked for a long while about the strange things that I had experienced over the past week, and Karia told Juna and me about all that she had been doing and learning at the willow. Juna just listened. He had not been a part of all that had gone on, but was actually quite interested in the whole story. I was relieved to finally know for sure that everything that had happened and I thought I dreamt was real, and that I was not alone. We spoke freely now, without the tension of the elders being around. We talked about the land sale, and shared information that we each had gathered, and then Karia told us about the elderly couple and the passing of the old woman. We all sat silently as she announced this sad news.

"Someone must convince the old man not to sell this precious land to those humans," Juna said, breaking the silence.

"I do not believe it is as simple as that," retorted Karia, still looking at the picture of Mim and Sire Argus.

"Why not?" I spoke up. "Why can't it be that simple? If these people are or were the kind of people you say they were, why do you think that the man won't listen to us?"

"Do you propose that we tell him about us, about Traegonia? That would surely cause our demise," Karia said, seeming shocked that I would suggest such a thing.

"No, we don't have to tell him anything about Traegonia. You said the old woman took care of all of the creatures of the forest, right? Well, I can approach it in that way," I answered back.

"You would talk to the man? By yourself?" questioned Karia, looking back over her shoulder, as if to see if we were being watched.

Dino C. Crisanti

Mim and Sire Argus

"Yeah, I would talk to him. Maybe he will listen to me. It's worth a try, don't you think?" I said, also looking around, but for what or who I didn't know. "Oh, I almost forgot, there is something else that my dad told my mom. He said that if we were able to find some rare or endangered plant or animal living in the forest, then the forestry people might consider purchasing the land themselves. Do you know of anything living here that is rare?" I asked, looking back and forth between Karia and Juna.

"Rare to whom? To the Traegons, all of the forest is rare and sacred, and deserves to be kept safe," Karia answered back.

In the distance, we heard my mom call, "Dino, Dino, it's time for lunch."

"Oh, shoot!" I said, looking quickly at my watch. "I'm late. I've got to go. I'll be back after lunch. Meet me back here, okay?"

"We will be here," said Karia and Juna together.

I jumped up and ran off in the direction of my mom's voice.

Chapter 19
The Unpuzzliers

Meanwhile, deep in the forest of Traegonia, Sir Antar had gone to see Bayalthazar, the leader of the Unpuzzliers. The Unpuzzliers were an odd group of eccentric inventers and profound thinkers. They created more than just ordinary, everyday items. They were charged with creating items that would benefit the community. Things that would help make life easier and aid them in their everyday living. Bayalthazar was a very tall and thin Traegon. His hair was white and kinky. Instead of glasses, he wore two eyepieces mounted on a metal band that he strapped around his head. He would flip one or both up and down as needed, which made his eye look extra-large when they were both flipped down. He wore what looked to be a gear, made into an earring, and had a couple of pouches that he wore on his hip.

Off in the back of his workshop, Bayalthazar had designed and built a large flying machine that was originally intended to assist in the location of concentrations of game for food, and further exploration of Traegon lands. The concept was similar to that of a hang glider, but the wings looked much like those of a large bat or bird. It had a tail that resembled a bird in flight that would move through a mechanism of small gears. As Antar and Bayalthazar stood looking over the magnificent flying machine,

Antar shared all that had gone on over the previous few days. He explained the urgency of the situation, and how everyone would work together on their individual tasks to find a solution to the problem at hand.

Sir Antar paused and looked at Bayalthazar. "Do you believe this flying machine could be used to gain additional information about the ones who seek to acquire this land?"

Bayalthazar looked proudly upon his creation and turned his gaze back to Antar. "You, my friend, know me better than any other. Have I ever been called to task and not created a way to make sure it happened?" Bayalthazar continued, "This flying machine has been tested and is able to move most discreetly through the skies without detection. I usually take it out at dawn or dusk, but in order to observe the activities of these humans, I believe it would be best to go out during the late morning. I will prepare this day, and set out tomorrow. I will retrieve any information I am able regarding the developers plans."

Sir Antar and Bayalthazar immediately began preparation for the mission. Rarely did the Unpuzzliers work in complete daylight and so close to humans. But these were special circumstances which called for extreme measures.

Dino C. Crisanti

Bayalthazar and Sir Antar

Chapter 20
The Petitions

I walked out of the woods and saw my mom talking with some other people in the park. She had a clipboard and was getting signatures on the petition she had drawn up. She had already gotten two pages of signatures, and wasn't having any trouble convincing people to sign. We met at the blanket and she seemed really pleased.

"Even though there are not a lot of people here, the ones that are definitely do not want to see this land taken away. Everyone would rather see it become part of the forest preserve," she shared with me, while she laid out lunch.

"That's really great, Mom," I replied.

Dad came up from the river and sat down. "I talked to some of the other guys who are fishing, and they weren't even aware of what is going on with the land. Anna, maybe you should come back down there with me after lunch. I know they will sign your petition," Dad said.

"Great, I will! But I'm not going to do any fishing." Mom smiled.

After lunch, Mom and Dad went down by the river and I went back into the woods to meet up with Karia and Juna. I had been thinking more about visiting with the elderly man and talking to him. I wondered if maybe I shouldn't tell my mother and ask her to take me there. But when I mentioned it to Karia, she didn't much like the idea.

"See here, Dino. It is stated within the prophecy that we will be the ones to resolve this situation," Karia said, very directly.

"Oh, I didn't really get that part," I responded, trying to remember exactly what the prophecy said.

"Well, it did. Now, I think that we should meet here tomorrow and you can take us to the edge of the forest. Then you can talk to the man while we stand guard," said Karia.

We made plans to meet back here tomorrow and go visit the elderly man. For the remainder of the afternoon, we read my journal, and Karia and Juna marveled at the pictures I had drawn. Karia shared more about her week, the willow and all that she had been learning. When she spoke of the garden, I began to recall what I had seen there that night. I decided to draw some of it as we visited. The day flew by, and it was time for me to go. We confirmed our plans for tomorrow and said goodbye for now.

Chapter 21
Council Meeting

J una returned home and Karia began her long journey back to the village of Traegonia, escorted by Oracle Balstar's raven, Sable. When she finally reached the village, it was late in the evening and she was tired. However, her day was not over yet. She was required to return to the willow garden to meet Balstar and the other council members to share all that they had learned over the past two days. All were deeply saddened at the news of the elderly woman's passing, which set a somber tone for the remainder of the meeting. Each again shared their stories of how the elderly couple had touched their lives. Madam Calthia shared yet another secret she had kept to herself for many years. After the woman had gifted her the wonderfully tasting pie, Calthia had returned and left a gift for the woman to show her appreciation for her kindness and generosity. Upon the windowsill where she had first seen the woman, she left a smooth pale pink stone, wrapped in a woven cloth that Calthia had made herself. She had tied it with a piece of sinew and attached a blue feather. The woman continued to help and care for all of nature for many years to come. Once the sharing and honoring of the woman had concluded, the remainder of the meeting ensued. Antar explained that Bayalthazar would go on the following day to the edge of Traegonia near the home of the elderly couple to try and obtain further information. Then it was Karia's turn. She had already decided not to inform the group of their plans to visit the elderly man for fear of being overruled, so she shared the information that Dino's father had gotten from the forestry division. If they could find a plant, tree, or animal that was considered rare or endangered, then the forestry division would step in and purchase the land for the sole purpose of protecting it. This would require much research because as far as the Traegons were concerned, all living things were deserving of protection.

Oracle Balstar appointed Master Zoal to look back through all of the recordings held by Traegonia, to locate documentation that might pertain to any living thing within their borders that might be considered worthy of protection by the humans. He instructed Bayalthazar to scour the forest boundaries for anything that might be in limited supply, as well as to keep an eye on the plans of the developer. The remaining council members were instructed to assist Master Zoal and Bayalthazar as needed, and wait for further instruction.

"Remember this, we must be diligent and work quickly as we really do not know how much time we have. You are all free to retire for the night, we will gather again in two nights."

Oracle Balstar looked tired and bent as he stood and left the room. One by one, everyone quietly followed.

Chapter 22
Preparing for a Journey

Karia had not slept well and found herself up very early the next morning. She lit some candles and began preparing for her journey, knowing that she had a great deal of traveling ahead of her. Suddenly, there was a knock on her door. This startled her because of the early hour, and she feared her plan had been found out. Karia slowly opened the door and peered out through the crack.

"Are you alright, dear?" a soft, kind, familiar voice asked. Karia opened the door and invited Para inside. "Yes, Para, I am just fine. What brings you out at such an early hour?"

"I saw the light flickering through your window and worried that there might be something amiss," Para answered. "What, may I ask, are you doing up at such an hour?"

"Para, may I confide in you without fear of others learning my words?" Karia asked in a secretive sort of way.

"Dear Karia, I am here as your attendant, to assist you in any way that I am able. Within reason that is," Para answered honestly.

"I will have to be gone from Traegonia this entire day, without anyone knowing that I am gone. I cannot tell you where I am going, but it will take me a long time to get there and back. All I ask of you is that if anyone asks of my whereabouts, you tell them that I am out seeking that which needs protecting. This is not a falsehood, Para. In many ways, this is exactly what I will be doing." Karia looked pleadingly into Para's eyes.

"Young one, I can see in your eyes that your heart is good and that you will not rest until you have accomplished your task. I will do as you ask. But how, may I ask, are you planning to travel?"

"Well, I haven't quite figured that out yet. I guess I hadn't thought that far ahead," Karia answered.

"Well, dear, that is a problem. I know a Squire who has a young turkey. I will inquire about a loan of his companion for the day. When will you be leaving?" Para questioned.

"Soon," answered Karia.

"Then I shall go now. I will meet you at the west end of the village shortly. That is the direction you will be heading? Yes?" Para asked.

"Yes and thank you!" Karia said, bowing her head.

Juna had informed Sire Argus and Mim that he would be going out to meet Dino and that he would return in time for the evening meal. I told my parents that I would be out riding my bike for the day, but would be home before dinner. We all met at the woods where we usually met. Karia bedded down the young turkey under a pine tree and made sure that there was enough food and water to keep him happy while we were gone. She told us of the meeting the night before. I had brought my empty book bag with me so that I could carry Karia and Juna on my bike. I hadn't figured the size quite right, so it was a pretty tight squeeze for the two of them. With each of them peering over my shoulders, we headed out in the direction of the elderly couple's home.

Chapter 23
An Unpuzzlier's Mission

The Unpuzzliers' workshop was set deep into a stone hill and Bayalthazar's takeoff and landing strip was hidden among the brush on top of the hill. In order to get enough height for takeoff, he needed additional assistance. Bayalthazar stood at the edge of the hill top, cupped his hands around his mouth, and let out a long, bird-like scream. Within moments, two hawks appeared in the sky heading straight for the hill top. They landed in front of Bayalthazar. "My good friends, your help once again is much appreciated." He tossed them each a mouse, which they promptly began to devour. While they ate, Bayalthazar cleared away the brush from his self-constructed runway. He then laid two ropes at the feet of the hawks and strapped himself into the flying machine. Bayalthazar squinted with determination, took a few deep breaths, and called to the hawks. They looked back at the flying machine, picked up the ropes in their talons, and took flight. At the same time, Bayalthazar began to run toward the edge of the top of the hill. Off he went. The hawks pulled him skyward until the air caught his wings and then he was flying. As he took a few practice maneuvers, the zee-ziet birds who occupied the treetops towering over and around the hill began taking turns dive-bombing the flying machine. They never took a liking to the flying machine, and were always causing Bayalthazar and the other Unpuzzliers trouble whenever he took the flyer out for a test run. These birds were blue and white, and it seemed they were most annoyed by the flying machine, especially during the time of their breeding season. The Traegons named them because of their high-pitched calls and songs.

As Bayalthazar got further from the hill, so did he from the zee-ziet birds. Armed with his map of Traegonia, he set off for the forest border. He kept the flying machine high enough that if any human spotted it, they would think it to be nothing more than an eagle or another large bird. On the rare occasion that humans had noticed the flying machine, they were quite curious and stared and pointed. Thankfully, Bayalthazar had been able to remain mostly unnoticed.

Once he had located the area of his targeted destination, he noticed that there was a car pulled off to the side of the road at the far end of the elderly couple's land, obscured from view. As he glided around, Bayalthazar could see two men leaning over the front of the car, looking at something. They would point at whatever was spread out on the hood of the car and then they would turn and point in different directions. Bayalthazar flipped down one of his eye pieces as he came around again to get a better view. All he could tell was that they were papers; he would have to land for a better look. He quietly glided in above the two men and located a small clearing where he set down just past where the two men stood.

Bayalthazar pushed his flying machine under a pine tree and slowly moved to another pine tree closer to where the two men were standing. He carefully and quietly climbed the trunk of the tree, concealed by the pine branches. He reached a branch that was just above the two men and began to climb quietly out onto the outstretched branch. Once in position, Bayalthazar flipped down the other eyepiece and focused the two of them together. Now he would be able to see what the two men were looking at. First, he saw a map with red circles on it.

Dino C. Crisanti

Bayalthazar's Flight

There were also other papers spread across the front of the car, and all of them had 'Billson Developers' printed across the top of them. *These must be the plans,* Bayalthazar thought to himself.

"I didn't expect this opposition to the project," Billson began as Bayalthazar hung quietly in the tree above them listening. "If we don't get the old man to sign soon, that woman and her kid could cause us more trouble than we bargained for. This could drag on for years."

"Do you think we should keep looking for other properties?" asked the other man.

"It wouldn't hurt, I suppose, but I really want this one. There's a lot of land here and at the price I put in the contract, we are getting it for a steal. We could build a super-mall and still have lots available for car dealerships, and a whole lot of other businesses. It could be the largest retail development anyone has ever seen. We could make a real lot of money on this one," Billson said, his eyes growing wide as he talked and dreamed.

"Won't it cost a lot to clear all of this land?" the other man asked, looking around at all of the trees and dense forest.

"If we get this land for the money I am offering, we can't lose. This guy has no idea what he has here. Nice for us, he is stupid and preoccupied with his dead wife. This is such a great time to get these people. All they want is to get away from their memories. Once they realize what they have done to themselves, it's too late. But you keep checking the obituaries, and if you find any other possible targets, let me know. It's not like these situations come along every day, so just keep your eyes open. I will work on pressuring the old man to make a commitment, sooner than later."

"Hey, Boss, I just had an idea. We could torch the land. Burn down all these trees and let the town do half our work. What do ya think?" the other man stated proudly.

"Ahh, my boy, now you're catching on." Billson smiled thoughtfully.

"Keep those ideas coming and we'll be the biggest thing this town has ever seen."

Bayalthazar listened closely and took in all that was said. He knew the two men were up to no good. He just didn't realize how demented and evil they were. A short while later, the two men packed up their papers, got into their car and drove away. Bayalthazar descended the tree and recovered his flying machine. He called out once again to the hawks and the two were there in moments. They soon had him in the sky and back on his way to Traegonia with his newfound information.

Chapter 24
Meeting Mr. Rhodes

We followed the river for a while and then rode through the forest as far as we could until it was just too thick to maneuver. Finally, I had to get onto the street for the rest of the ride. Karia and Juna had to crouch down inside the book bag once I reached the road so they wouldn't be seen. This made riding my bike tough. It felt like they were having a wrestling match inside my book bag. I know they didn't mean it, but they were pounding so hard on my back that I had to pull over and persuade them to sit still. I told them that we were almost there, and if they kept it up we would all have to walk the rest of the way. Well, they either knocked each other out, or decided that it would be better than walking.

Finally, we came upon a long gravel driveway that disappeared into the forest ahead. The driveway wound around, dropping us out in a clearing where a charming old white house stood amid the surrounding forest. It was beautiful. *What a great place to live,* I thought. I just couldn't imagine anyone wanting to tear this place down. I walked my bike to the edge of the forest and laid it down. I pulled off my heavy book bag, gently laid it on the ground and pulled it open. Both Karia and Juna scrambled to get out as fast as they could. They wedged themselves in the opening of the bag, making it impossible for either of them to gain their freedom.

"Wait a minute, you two! Come out of there one at a time."

I held the bag open and Juna backed out feet first with Karia following closely behind. They looked as if they had been, well, stuffed in a book bag.

"You both wait over here in the bushes while I go and see if the man will even talk to me. I'll be back as soon as I can."

As I walked toward the front of the house, I noticed a car and an old pick-up truck parked on the far side of the house. I wondered if the car might belong to the developer. I walked up the front steps, reached out and rang the doorbell. Moments later, the door opened and a woman about my mom's age appeared.

"Can I help you?" she asked.

"Um, yes," I said. "Are you the person who lives here?" I asked, trying to see around her for the elderly man.

"And who are you?" she asked kindly.

"Oh, I'm sorry. My name is Dino. I wanted to talk to the man who lives here."

The woman stepped back into the house and called out, "Dad, there's a young boy here, he says he wants to talk to you."

I looked back over my shoulder to see if I could see Karia and Juna, but they were well hidden.

"Yes, can I help you?" a voice growled.

When I turned back around, I saw a thin old man looking at me through the screen door. "What do you want, boy? I've had more strangers come to my door in the last two weeks than I have the whole time I've lived here," he grumbled, seeming to get annoyed at me quickly.

"Sir, my name is Dino, and if you wouldn't mind, I really need to talk to you about the people who want to buy your land."

The man just stared at me as if I were from another planet. I even looked down to make sure I didn't have something on the front of my shirt. "Please, sir, it's really important."

The screen door swung open and the man stretched out his arm, holding the door open and directing me to enter. "Come in. What did you say your name was?"

"Dino, sir," I answered politely, as I stepped through the door. Immediately, I could smell pie-apple pie, I think.

"Is that like the actor or the dog?" he asked rather seriously.

"Dad, stop that! Be nice," the woman reprimanded as she entered the living room with two glasses of lemonade on a tray.

"Hi, I'm Sara. Sorry about my dad."

"That's okay, I think I have heard them all," I said, smiling at her.

She placed a glass in front of me and one in front of her father. "This is my father, Mr. Rhodes."

"I can speak for myself, Sara, and you don't need to apologize for me. I'm sure the boy can take a joke. Jim Rhodes, you can call me Jim. Now, what was it that you wanted to talk to me about?"

"Excuse me, I'm going to get back to my pies. It was nice meeting you, Dino." Sara smiled and walked back into the kitchen.

"Well, sir, I mean Jim. My family and I heard about your wife and we are really sorry." I paused.

"Thank you, Dino, I appreciate your condolences. But you said something about the land sale."

"Um yes, sir, well, I just think you should know that there are some people who are very sad that these developers are going to tear down this beautiful forest. And well, I was hoping that maybe I could change your mind." I felt very nervous and that everything I was saying wasn't making much sense.

The old man took a deep breath. "Well, young man, I will be going to live with my daughter out of state. Now that my wife is gone, there isn't much reason for me to stay. This was her dream house; she loved it here." He paused and swallowed hard. "But now, well, I just can't stay here anymore."

"I do understand, sir. Would it be OK if I called you sir? It's just how I was taught."

"Of course, and I'll just call you boy." He smiled and took a sip of his lemonade. "Shortly after my wife passed on, this man knocked on my door and offered to buy this property. It's a lot of land, and I was concerned about how I was going to be able to sell it all. The visit seemed like an answer to a prayer."

"Yes, sir, I understand, but I met this man with my mother one day, and we just got the idea that he didn't have the best of intentions. Did you know he wants to tear down this house and a lot of the forest? He wants to build a shopping mall," I told him.

"Look, Dino, I understand why you are upset. I don't think we need any more malls either, but who else is going to buy this much land? I don't have much time to make a decision, that's why my daughter is here. We need to go over the contract before we sign it."

"Please, sir, maybe you could wait just a little longer before you make a decision. Maybe you could try putting an ad in the paper, or a sign up and see if there might be someone else who would love this land, like you and your wife did," I pleaded.

"Do you know something you're not telling me? Why are you so interested in this deal anyway? You sure seem to have a lot of information for such a young boy," Mr. Rhodes questioned.

"No, sir, I just don't think that your wife would have wanted this land destroyed," I responded.

"What do you know about my wife anyway?" Mr. Rhodes snapped. "Who are you to come here and think that you can solve my problems, or even understand my situation?" He seemed to become more and more agitated.

"I'm sorry, sir. I don't mean to upset you." I felt that if I didn't do something soon, he would ask me to leave. I thought of something Karia had told me about one of the meetings with the council members. "Sir, I'm going to tell you something, but I cannot tell you how I know this. Please, just listen."

I moved to the edge of my seat and leaned in. "A long time ago, your wife received a small pink stone wrapped in a cloth pouch. The cloth was tied with a small piece of twine and had a blue feather tied onto it. It was a gift to her for her kindness to all of the living things of the forest."

The man just sat staring at me. "Boy, I don't know how you know these things." Mr. Rhodes' voice quieted as he looked down, scratched his head, and continued. "I know of this thing, this 'gift' you're talking about. I found something like that in her jewelry box. I don't know where she got it, but she kept it with some things our daughter gave her when she was a child. So I just figured it was from Sara."

"If you could just wait another week or so before you agree to sell to the developer. Please, just a little while longer. There are some people who are working very hard to make sure this land doesn't fall into the wrong hands. We know you want to leave here, but I think that if you ever come back, you wouldn't want to see a mall where your house once stood. I really think that things will work out," I pleaded with him.

————))(()((————

While Dino was in the house talking to Mr. Rhodes, Karia was telling Juna about the last time she had been here with Arbalest. She told him about the hanging planter and the dried up old flowers. She suggested that they could plant some new flowers in honor of the old woman. Karia had come prepared, telling Juna that she had brought some seeds and some water from Oracle Balstar's fountain in the garden.

K.S. KRUEGER

"Come on, Juna. We'll just plant these and we'll come right back," Karia said persuasively. Juna reluctantly agreed and they made their way across the yard to the back porch. Karia found the pot. It was sitting on a table on the back porch. She pulled out the last of the dried up flowers and mixed the dirt with her hands. She reached into the pouch tied around her waist, pulling out a wooden jar and a small pouch of seeds.

She carefully laid the seeds in the hole she had made in the center of the dirt and gently covered them. She then removed the cork from the jar and poured the water over them. Karia asked Juna to help her to invoke the positive, healing energies over the seeds, as they had done at the tree in the forest. Placing their hands over the barren pot and closing their eyes, they began the prayer.

"Tiny seeds of tomorrow, carefully planted with love,
Nurtured by the purest rain and light from above.
Bring forth your beauty for all to see,
Growing tall and strong, let it be."

As they opened their eyes, they were amazed at how quickly the tiny sprouts had pushed their way through the moist dirt. Juna looked at Karia and they both smiled. Just then, Juna's nose caught a sweet scent wafting through the air. "What is that delicious scent?" he asked, turning back to Karia.

Karia sniffed at the air and smelled it too. "Pie? Maybe it is the pie that Madam Calthia spoke of."

"It seems to be coming from over here," Juna said, as he began to walk toward the side of the house.

"Juna, we should get back to the forest now. We cannot risk being caught," Karia said, trying to ignore the tempting scent.

Juna didn't seem to hear anything that Karia said, he was too busy following the scent to an open window, where a sweet pie rested upon the sill, cooling. Karia turned to find Juna standing beneath the window with his mouth open and his nose in the air. He looked completely mesmerized.

"Juna," Karia whispered. "What are you doing? We are going to be seen."

"I just want a taste, just a small taste. It has been a long morning, and I am really getting hungry. Besides, do you not want to know what this pie thing tastes like?" Juna pleaded with Karia, without ever taking his eyes off of the pie.

Karia took another deep breath of the wonderful scent, and agreed. "Just one small taste."

Juna smiled and instructed Karia to boost him up.

"Together, we are still not tall enough to reach the windowsill," Karia pointed out, looking around for something that they could stand on. She spotted a wooden trellis, lying in the weeds near the house.

"Wait here, I will return immediately," she told Juna, who was still staring up at the open window, his mouth hanging open. Karia returned quickly, dragging the trellis behind her. "Here, help me to stand this upright." Juna turned and noticed Karia struggling with the trellis.

"Very good! That will work nicely," he said, as he helped her prop it up against the house. "You hold it steady while I climb up."

"Don't forget to bring some back for me," Karia said, as she steadied the makeshift ladder. "And be careful not to be seen."

When Juna reached the window, the sill protruded out above his head. He had to lean back a bit in order to grab onto it. He almost lost his balance, and the way he was holding on didn't offer him much opportunity to make sure that he wouldn't be seen. The scent of the pie seemed to give him the extra strength to pull himself up. As he cleared the sill, he could see Sara standing in the doorway with her back to the window, listening to the conversation between Dino and her father. Juna figured he could get some pie and descend the trellis before she turned around. He swung one of his legs up onto the sill and reached up with his free hand, grabbing the edge of the pie plate. Right at that moment, Sara turned around. Juna became startled and lost his balance. As he fell, he pulled the pie plate down with him. Juna landed on his back and the pie splattered all over the ground, Karia, and himself.

The commotion could be heard all the way into the living room, where Jim and I were sitting. We quickly rushed into the kitchen.

"Are you all right?" Jim asked, concerned for his daughter.

Sara turned around with a look of disbelief on her face. "Uh, I'm fine. My…my pie! It must have been a raccoon or something. It just pulled it right out the window," she murmured, kind of unsure of herself.

"A raccoon, this time of the day?" her father questioned.

My stomach turned. *Karia and Juna,* I thought. I walked over to the window and looked out, hoping that if it was them, I would give them time to get away. When I looked out the window, I saw the splattered pie on the ground. Three squirrels and some birds were enjoying what was left. I shook my head. Then I called Jim and Sara over to see.

"Well, they really seem to be enjoying your pie," I said. Jim and Sara joined me at the window and looked out. The sight cast smiles across both of their faces.

"Come on, boy. Let's take a walk," Jim said, as he turned and headed for the back porch. "Look, I will hold off on giving the developer an answer for two weeks. We will see what happens between now and then," Jim conceded in a kinder voice, as we stepped onto the porch.

"Thank you, sir. I know you won't be sorry." I thanked him for talking to me and thanked Sara for the lemonade. She was starting another pie, still looking a bit puzzled.

"Oh, that's okay," she said, "nice to meet you."

I stepped off the porch and headed back to the front where my bike was. I looked back and waved to Jim and he waved to me. Then he turned around to go back into the house, not without noticing the hanging planter sitting on the small table, complete with five fresh blooms.

"Did you plant some new flowers, Sara?" Jim hollered into the house.

"No, Dad, not since I've been here," she responded.

Jim looked around his back yard and at the beautiful woods that surrounded his home. He shook his head, smiled, and walked back into the house.

I walked across the yard toward my bike, keeping my eyes open for any sign of Karia and Juna. They were nowhere in sight. When I reached my bike, I noticed what seemed to be traces of apple pie on the leaves leading into the forest. I glanced back and saw Jim and Sara standing in the window. In a low whisper, I called to Karia and Juna. "If you two can hear me, stay in the woods and meet me down the driveway out of sight of the house."

A muffled call responded back, "OK, Dino."

Once down the driveway and out of sight of the house, I pulled my bike into the woods and waited. Karia and Juna appeared, sticky with apple pie and a few flying insects enjoying their mishap.

"Oh, that's just great. Look at you two. I knew it was you. You know, I think she saw you. I know she saw something." I noticed that I sounded a little like my mother as I reprimanded them. "How am I supposed to put the two of you in my book bag like this?" I asked, trying to figure out what to do next. As I looked around the forest, I spotted an old plastic tarp lying off in the distance. I walked over to have a better look.

The tarp was crumpled next to what looked to be an old woodpile.

When I picked it up, a few mice scurried off. It was pretty beat up and shredded across the center. I figured it would be all right to tear some off since it seemed the only ones making use of it were the mice, and I would still leave plenty for them. I found the shredded area and pulled hard toward the bottom corner. A good-sized piece tore free, and I walked back to where I had left Karia and Juna. The two of them were still sitting preoccupied with being covered with pie, and being swarmed with gnats and flies, which seemed to keep increasing in number. My thought was to just get them back to the river so that we could get them cleaned up, and then try to get home before my parents got suspicious. I tucked the tarp into my back pack and helped Karia and Juna squeeze in. It was a tight fit on the way here, but now with the tarp, it was almost impossible. I rode as fast as I could down the road and back through the forest to the river. Finally, after a long and very uncomfortable ride for Karia and Juna, we were at the river. They quickly squeezed themselves out of the bag and climbed right into the water. Juna didn't complain once. I think we were all tired from our long day; I know I was.

"This has been a very eventful day, don't you think?" Karia said, popping out of the water. "Were you able to get him to change his mind about selling the property?"

"I was able to get him to wait before making any decision. Hopefully, we've bought ourselves a little more time," I responded. "It's getting late. I'm gonna have to get home before my parents get worried. It's going to start to get dark soon."

"You are right, I had better begin back, I have quite a journey ahead of me," Karia agreed.

Karia and Juna dried themselves off and retrieved the wild turkey from under the bush where we had left it. They said their goodbyes and Karia climbed into the wagon, heading off in the opposite direction. Juna looked a bit sad to see her go.

"Well, I had better return home as well. I guess we will be seeing you soon. Take care." Juna put his hand up, turned, and headed off down the trail.

I picked up my bike and when I looked back, they were both gone. I got on my bike and rode home as fast as I could.

Chapter 25
Alone in the Woods

The sun retreated quickly and the forest grew dark. Karia began to feel as if she was not completely sure of the way. She had hoped that the turkey would remember some of the way, but knew that they were not the brightest fowl in the forest. She pulled a lantern from the back of the wagon and lit the large candle inside, then hung it on a lantern pole at the front of the wagon. She was becoming a bit unnerved as she looked at the path before her. She began to hum to ease her concern. She came to a split in the path and stopped, looking at each new trail. She just could not be sure which trail would lead her back to the village. She heard a noise that startled her. She looked around trying to see what it was. It sounded like something scurrying through the leaves. *A rabbit, perhaps,* she thought to herself. Then another sound came from above her, in the trees. She looked again at the trails before her. Her heart began to pound and she quickly decided. She pulled the reins to the right and snapped them hard. The turkey knew one thing; she meant business. He pulled forward fast and headed up the trail. Beyond the noise of the wagon, she could still hear something moving quickly through the trees behind her. There were always noises in the forest at night, but she also knew that there were certain predators that would be bold enough to attack a Traegon. Whatever it was could also be after her steed.

But from the trees, what predator could move through the trees with such agility and speed? Karia's mind raced as she pressed the turkey to move as fast as he could. Suddenly, he came to an abrupt halt. Thinking the turkey and she had come face-to-face with the predator, she took a deep breath as she steadied herself in the wagon. To her surprise, there before her was another split in the trail. She had been moving so fast, she hadn't been paying attention to where she was. She hadn't seen any trail markings guiding her way. It was completely dark now and she wasn't even sure how long she had been traveling. Now she was sure of only one thing; she was definitely lost.

Karia listened for a moment… nothing. Had she lost the predator, or was it waiting to attack? She had to calm herself in order to think clearly about what she should do next. Something landed on the wagon and startled her, she turned quickly ready to defend herself, but to her surprise it wasn't a predator at all. It was Sable, Oracle Balstar's raven, and another smaller raven.

"How glad I am to see you. How did you find me? Have you been following me the whole time? Does Oracle Balstar know I am gone? I was becoming quite nervous." Sable just sat staring at Karia. "Well, do something," Karia snapped. Sable stood quietly, waiting for Karia to stop speaking. He looked directly into her eyes and she looked back, and suddenly, the words poured into her head. Sable wasn't speaking to her through voice, but she clearly knew what he wanted her to know.

"Para was worried, said it was late, getting dark; wasn't sure if you were safe. Asked me to come, follow me! I will lead you back to the village."

All of this Karia heard in her thoughts as Sable looked patiently into her eyes. *How is this possible?* She had to be sure she wasn't just making this up in her own thoughts, so she repeated; "I should follow you and you will lead me back to the village?" The smaller crow in the back of the wagon cawed and shook his body, and then flew into the air. Karia looked back at Sable. He too cawed and flew out of the wagon, circled around once in front of her, and then cawed again.

"Alright, you lead," Karia said. Karia snapped the reins and the turkey began to follow. Soon, she saw the great willow in the distance, the moonlight glistening off of the massive tree top. Karia took a deep breath, relieved that she was finally back. She stopped the wagon and waited for Sable to land on the seat next to her.

"Thank you, I owe you much gratitude. I know I would not have made it back without you." Karia looked into Sable's eyes. She reached into her pocket and pulled out a handful of her Mim's Traegon mix and held out her hand. Sable took it gently and shook his head. Suddenly, the other crow landed on the front of the wagon and flapped his wings. Karia turned and offered some to him as well. "Thank you both again," They flapped their wings and flew off toward the willow.

Karia made her way back to the willow and was greeted by Para. "You have been gone longer than I had expected you would be. I was beginning to worry. I was going to go to Oracle Balstar if you did not return soon. I am glad you are back."

"I too am glad to be back. It has been a very long journey," Karia responded.

Para motioned and a Squire approached to take the wagon away. Para helped Karia to her room and then helped her to bed. Karia was asleep as soon as she lay down.

Chapter 26
Searching for an Answer

The next morning, I woke with a renewed sense of relief. We would have a few more weeks to find a way to keep Mr. Billson from purchasing the Traegons' land. I went downstairs to find my mother sitting at the kitchen table, reading over a stack of books.

"What are those?" I asked, as I looked through the cabinets for something to eat.

"I'm trying to find out what types of plants or animals might be considered endangered in this area. I'm going to go out into the forest over the next week and see if I can find anything. I figure if I can create a list with pictures and descriptions, I just might be able to find something. I know it's a long shot, but I can't sit around hoping that it will work itself out. I'm also going to stop by the Department of Natural Resources," she said, as she thumbed through the pages of the books, marking pages with paper. "I'm going to be spending a lot of time working on this over the next few weeks, so I will need you to be patient with me if I'm not home as much as I usually am. Do you understand?"

"Sure, Mom. I want to help too. Maybe I could meet you over there after school a couple of days. Maybe Quinn will want to come too."

"We'll have to see how things go, and how much homework you have. But I appreciate your offer and I will keep it in mind."

I finished my breakfast and headed off to school. I couldn't stop thinking about what my mother said, endangered, something that needs protection. All I could think of was the Traegons. But I knew I must keep their secret. There must be something else out there. *I will have to talk more to Karia about this.*

That afternoon when I got home from school, my mother wasn't there. *She must be at the woods,* I thought. There was a note on the table with instructions to start dinner. I took out my books and sat at the table to do my homework. I had a little time before I had to start dinner.

Chapter 27
Karia's New Friend

Karia slept in a bit, exhausted from her long journey the day before. Para knocked at her door, bearing a meal fit for a queen. "Good day, my dear. I hope you were able to sleep well. Come and put something in your stomach so that you may regain your strength."

Karia walked over to the small table and sat down. She took a few bites and sat quietly.

"Was your journey productive?" Para inquired.

"I believe it was. We have procured a bit more time to work on a solution to the community's plight." Karia spoke softly. "I hope the endeavors of the others have been fruitful as well. Tonight, we meet again to share our discoveries. I think I will take a walk through the village later to clear my thoughts."

"That sounds like a nice idea," Para agreed.

Karia finished her morning meal, dressed, and headed out into the village. It was quiet during the daylight hours; the village bustled only at dawn and at dusk. Although there were a few Traegons out and about during the light hours, Karia was able to walk quietly and thoughtfully. She thought about Mim and Sire Argus. She missed them both terribly, and wondered when she might be able to see them again. Karia walked to the edge of Mazus Grove and sat on a small log lying along the water's edge.

She looked off into the distance above the trees. She closed her eyes and fell into a sort of dream state.

Suddenly, she heard a high-pitched, "Gick, gick, gick." She opened her eyes and looked around. She carefully scanned the edge of the bog for any sign of what might have made the sound, but she saw nothing. She sat very quietly listening for another sound or any other movement that might indicate she wasn't alone but she heard nothing. She closed her eyes again and tried to still her thoughts. Moments later, she heard a loud high-pitched single gick. This time, she opened only one eye, hoping to catch a glimpse of the creature who was taunting her. Again, she saw nothing. There were tall grasses that grew along the edge of the bog with patches of open mud that led into the water. The Royal Fern field stretched out beyond the water. The grasses there grew quite tall, so it made a perfect place for small creatures to remain well-hidden.

Becoming a bit annoyed, Karia said, "Who intends to disturb my quiet time? If you need something from me, then state your purpose, otherwise, please let me be."

Karia waited for some type of response. None came. She closed her eyes again and quieted her thoughts. She began to see her family in her mind's eye. She saw Mim cooking in their humble tree home, and Sire Argus sitting before the fire, building something to sell at the market. She watched in her thoughts as Juna brought in some herbs for Mim, and more branches for the fire. Karia felt joy in her being. She felt as if she was there with them. Once she completed her vision, she opened her eyes and to her surprise, there was a small frog sitting before her. He just sat there watching her.

"Hello, who are you?" Karia asked kindly.

"Gick-gick!" the frog replied.

"Oh, aren't you cute! Are you the one who interrupted my quiet time earlier?" Karia asked.

"Gick-gick-gick," the frog replied.

"Well, at least you're honest. I have to be going now, but it was a pleasure to make your acquaintance."

Karia stood and walked back toward the willow. She could hear something hopping through the grass and mud behind her, and when she turned around, there was the little frog, just sitting there, looking at her. He followed her all the way back to the willow. When they reached her door, she asked him, "Don't you think you should return to your family?"

The frog glanced to the ground and gave a sad sounding, "Gick."

"Well, I sense that you may need some help returning home, but I have some very important business to attend to first. You are welcome to stay with me for a while, and then tomorrow I will help you get home." Karia opened the door and the two entered her room.

Karia prepared for the meeting with the council members. She went to Oracle Balstar prior to the meeting. She requested that they call Dino to attend, as they together, had information that could prove invaluable. Oracle Balstar approved and instructed Karia to join him early in the garden, to summon Dino before the start of the meeting. Karia went back to her room and had her evening meal a bit early, with her new friend quietly in tow. He followed her everywhere, but was hardly noticed as he would sit quietly and wait as she went about her business. Finally, it was time to meet Oracle Balstar in the garden. Karia and her new friend were prompt and they waited for Oracle Balstar to arrive. Karia stood before the stone circle, thinking about going to get Dino. It was definitely an interesting experience, but also a bit unnerving. Her little frog friend sat at a distance behind her, and went unnoticed when Oracle Balstar appeared.

Karia stepped into the circle as she had done before. She closed her eyes and breathed deeply, listening to her heartbeat. She was suddenly falling through time and space, landing in the corner of Dino's room. Karia quickly woke Dino and they returned promptly to the garden.

————)(◉)(————

Once we stepped out of the circle, Oracle Balstar spoke. "Dino, it is good to see you again! Karia tells me you have some important information to share at the meeting."

"Yes, Oracle, I hope that I can be of help tonight," I responded.

"Karia, why did you not introduce me to your friend before you left?" Balstar looked back over his shoulder.

Karia looked at the ground slightly behind Balstar. There sitting quietly was the little frog.

"Oh, I apologize. He is so quiet I sometimes forget he is there," replied Karia. "He found me near Mazus Grove earlier, and has followed me around ever since. I am going to help him find his way home tomorrow."

Just then, the rest of the group entered the garden and began to take their places at a table near the pond. Once they were all seated, attention was directed to Karia and I. "Karia has informed me that she and Dino have some new information," Oracle Balstar addressed the council. "Karia, you may proceed."

Karia stood, looked at me, took a deep breath, and began to address the group. "Please listen before you respond. We would greatly appreciate completing our story before you share your thoughts on our choices."

The group looked at each other and then back at Karia. They had that look as if to say, "What have you done now?"

Karia proceeded, "We met with the elderly man yesterday."

A gasp was heard from the far end of the table. When Karia and I looked in that direction, we could see the Madam's looking a bit shocked.

"Dino felt if we spoke to him directly, he might wait a bit before making his decision. As it turns out, he was to meet with the developer on this day. It is a good thing we wasted no time. He had knowledge of the gift given to his wife by Madam Calthia. I think this information was crucial in getting him to understand our seriousness, and allow us a bit more time before he agrees to the contract with the developer."

"Now we just have to find a way to keep this land from being destroyed." I stood and continued, "My mother has started doing research into anything that might be endangered in this area. She is going to go to the forest and begin looking for any signs of these species in order to try and have this land protected by the government."

"Dino, I understand your family has a fondness for this park that borders this land, but why would she put so much effort into the protection of this land? Have you spoken to her of our existence?" questioned Sir Pexor.

I responded, feeling a bit irritated that my promise was being questioned, "We, I mean my family and I, love the forest preserve that borders this land. We have been coming here for as long as I can remember, and we don't feel that there needs to be any more land destroyed for buildings, especially land that is filled with so many old and wonderful trees and wildlife. This is your home, and that is more of a reason for me to want to help, but my mother just has a great respect for the land and the plants and animals that live here."

Everyone was silent for a moment. Then Madam Shoran spoke. "I can sense in your voice protection for your mother. You must be very close to her?"

"Yes, I am," I responded, hoping that I hadn't offended anyone with my tone. "But even though I am close to my mother, I still made a promise to Karia and Juna, and I intend to keep that promise. At least, until or if ever you direct me otherwise."

Karia placed her hand on my arm and told me, "I do not question your intentions, and I know in my heart that your promise is strong and honorable."

I smiled at her and appreciated her trust in me.

"I think we can all take comfort in that," said Madam Taendia.

I continued, "The man told me that he is going to live with his daughter, but that he would wait two more weeks before giving his answer to the developers."

"The child," Madam Calthia whispered. "Did you see her? I remember when she was young and would play in the yard. She also loved the animals and the flowers."

"Yes, I saw her. Her name is Sara. She was very nice and she was making pies when I was there," I responded to Calthia. "But she is all grown up now. The important thing is that we have some more time." I sat back down.

Oracle Balstar spoke. "It was a brave thing you did to go there on your own. It is fortunate things turned out in a good way. We would only request that all plans be made known to the council. I probably would have sent Arbalest with you. Karia, you should not be traveling alone. It is not safe."

"I apologize, Oracle. I was just concerned you would not let us go," Karia said.

"You must trust me. I will always carefully consider your words, as your part in this has been laid out in the prophecy,"

Oracle Balstar stated. "Now, what other information have we gained in the short time since we met last?"

"I have found nothing in the scrolls that speaks to any one thing that Traegonia has intended to protect. We have always only used what was necessary, and allowed time for the replenishment of our resources. The scrolls state that all creatures are to be respected and allowed their space to live and flourish," Master Zoal stated. "Though I will continue to search for more information."

"Does anyone else have additional information to share?" questioned Balstar.

Bayalthazar stood. He began to divulge his findings. He explained how the developer, Mr. Billson, would seek out people who were vulnerable, people who had something that he wanted, and he would make it look like he was doing them a favor, and in this case, someone who was distraught over the loss of his wife. He explained how they were planning to make one of the largest malls anyone had ever seen, which would mean clearing most, if not all of the land. He even shared with them how they searched the obituaries in the newspapers in order to find targets for their schemes. "They were still looking for others." he concluded.

The council members, Oracle Balstar, and Karia were all outraged at the methods the developer had chosen to procure land. Sir Pexor stated in an angry voice, "There is nothing, not even the lowest grub that could compare to the slimy tactics this one has chosen! To wait like a vulture circling the weak, until he seizes his opportunity to devour all that one has left. This kind of evil cannot and will not be tolerated."

This information only served to empower the group even more. The Madam's were sickened by the information about the developer and his deceitful practices. "He must be stopped, not only for our sake but for the well-being of all he will eventually harm," stated Madam Shoran.

Bayalthazar continued, "The Unpuzzliers have been working on a second flying machine. In light of the information received on this night, we will begin working on adapting this flying machine in order to make it so that two may fly together. This will allow us the ability for one to keep a closer watch, while the other maneuvers the flyer to seek out any creatures that we may be looking for. I request that Dino bring us any information he can to guide our search. We must have something to seek before we are able to find it."

"Excellent! Any others?" asked Oracle Balstar.

Sir Antar questioned, "Due to our need to find a creature that the humans deem worthy of protection, do you suppose we should call a community meeting, to share what we know to allow others the opportunity to assist us? After all, we are just a small group."

"I cannot be sure this would be a wise idea. I am still concerned that we may instead cause a panic among the community, and that would hinder our cause, not help it," answered Oracle Balstar. "I will think on this, though, and we can address it at our next convening." Oracle Balstar looked around the room. "Now if there are no more thoughts on the matter, I will not set a specific time that we will next meet, but I ask you all to be available at a moment's notice if necessary. Please continue to uncover any plans or ideas that will serve to benefit our situation. You are all dismissed."

Karia and I stood and excused ourselves as the others continued to discuss other matters. We walked toward the circle and spoke softly, the small frog followed silently. "Well, Dino, it is time for you to return to your world now," said Karia.

"Yeah, I know. What do you think we should do next?" I asked quietly.

"Well, I know that the first thing I must to is return this

little guy back to his home," Karia said, looking down at the little frog.

"Where do you think he came from?" I asked her, kneeling down on one knee to take a closer look. "He really is small, and kinda different looking. I don't know if I would ever notice him at my normal size."

"I suppose," said Karia, as if not really paying attention. "I guess we should come up with a plan to find this, as you say, endangered creature."

"Hopefully, my mom will have something more tomorrow," I told her.

"I think I will try to go and visit Juna, Mim, and Sire Argus, and tell them what we have found. Maybe they can help. Maybe they know of something," Karia said.

"That's a good idea. I will go to the woods on the weekend. Can you meet me there?"

"Yes, I will ask Juna to come as well," Karia responded.

We stepped into the circle, I looked Karia in the eyes, and we moved to the center and sat down. "See you soon," I told her and we closed our eyes, took a deep breath and tumbled through time. I was asleep as soon as I landed.

Dino C. Crisanti

Little Frog in the Willow Garden

Chapter 28
Just What They're Looking For

Morning came fast. I felt tired but the distant calls from my mom urged me to get up. "Dino, come on now! I have called you five times!" I opened my eyes and blinked hard, rolled over and blinked again, and then saw the little frog sitting beside my head on the pillow.

"What are you doing here?" I asked, surprised to see him. "Karia is going to be worried about you."

The little frog just sat quietly, staring at me, and blinking every few seconds. "Well, I am going to have to find a temporary home for you until we see Karia again. You're so small you could get stepped on." I got up, got dressed, and pulled a shoebox down from my closet shelf. I dumped out a lot of little things I had collected. "This will have to do for now." The frog sat patiently on my pillow, watching, and waiting. "You are really a strange little guy, you know?" I said, looking at the frog as he seemed to watch and wait for me to finish what I was doing. I prepared the box with holes in the top and figured I would get some grass from outside until I could find out what a frog habitat should be like. I carried the box into the bathroom while I washed my face and brushed my hair. I turned on the water and began to wash my face when suddenly, the little frog hopped out of the box, landed on the edge of the sink, and slid into the water. I quickly turned off the water and pushed down the drain.

"What are you doing?" I said, startled and afraid he might slip down the drain. I carefully placed the wet frog into the box and set the lid on tight, then I grabbed my backpack, put my books and homework in it and tossed it over my shoulder. I grabbed the shoebox, put it under my arm, and went downstairs for breakfast.

My mom was in the kitchen. She had just finished making my lunch when I came in and sat down at the table. "Good morning, honey, did you sleep well?" she asked, turning around as I set the shoebox on the table.

"I guess so," I said, pouring some cereal into the bowl she had waiting for me on the table.

Mom walked to the refrigerator, took out the milk, and brought it over to where I was sitting. "What's in the box?" she asked, pouring the milk into my bowl. I was too tired and hadn't really thought of what I was going to tell her about where I had found him. But I knew I couldn't tell her the truth. "It's a frog," I said, and left it at that.

"A frog? Where on earth did you get it?" she asked me with a puzzled look on her face.

"Um, I went to the woods yesterday after school to see if you were there, but I couldn't find you so I just came home. He must have hopped into my backpack when I set it on the ground. I didn't notice him until late last night. I found him on the floor next to my backpack," I explained, making it up as I went along.

"I didn't know you were in the woods yesterday. Why didn't you say something?" she asked, puzzled.

"I didn't think it was important, since I couldn't find you and I didn't stay long anyway. Did you have any luck?" I asked, trying desperately to change the subject.

"No, not much, it's really going to be a big job. I was pretty overwhelmed when I got to the woods and looked at just how big it was. A lady at the DNR office said she would have a list of protected and endangered species for me, at the end of the week. She was more than happy to sign my petition, and even told me that it doesn't have to be just animals or birds. She said there are endangered and protected plants, insects, and fish as well. I think I may have to go deeper into the woods to find anything that hasn't already been found if there is anything out there. Maybe you, Quinn, and your dad could come with me this weekend and we could all search together. This is much too big a job for just one person." She looked at the box again. "Can I see your frog?"

"Uh, sure," I said, lifting the lid. "Can I get a copy of the information you get from the DNR so I can read it before we go? Then we can split up," I said, thinking about giving it to the elders.

Mom looked in the box. "Oh, how cute is he. He is so tiny, I'm surprised you even saw him before stepping on him. Do you have any idea of how to take care of him? You can't just keep him in a shoebox, you know."

"I know. I am going to put some grass in here and look him up on the computer after school. I should be able to find something about him there."

"You can't just leave him in a box all day while you are at school," she told me, concerned for his well-being. "How do you know when he has eaten last? Do you want me to take him back to the woods with me and let him go?"

"NO!" I stopped myself. I couldn't tell her that I had to bring him back to Karia, but I also couldn't let her go and release him either. "I mean, I kind of like him. I think I would like to see if I can keep him for a while. I promise I will take care of him. Can I keep him for a little while? If I can't figure out how to take care of him, I will release him at the woods this weekend. It's only a few more days. Please?" I begged her.

"Oh all right, but leave him here. I'll run to the library this morning and see if I can look up any information on the computer there. He's probably going to need to eat something soon," she said.

"Thanks, Mom. I really appreciate it. I'll fix him a nice home when I get back after school. Maybe you could bring home some sticks and dried leaves when you go to the woods today," I suggested, picking up my backpack and heading toward the door.

"Oh, I see! 'I promise I'll take care of him.' How does it always become Mom's job!" She smiled.

"Thanks, Mom. I really will take care of him, I just gotta go now." I kissed her on the cheek and walked out the door.

After Dino left, Anna went back to the table, sat down and looked at the frog again. "So, what is it that you like to eat, huh?" She leaned over the box and looked closely at the very tiny frog. "You really are different. We'll have to find out a bit more about you." She cleaned up the kitchen, grabbed her purse and the shoebox, and headed off to the library.

The library wasn't far from the house, and was on the way to the forest where she was planning to go anyway. She pulled up in front of the old two-story library, parked in the two-hour parking space and walked up the old concrete steps to the large white double doors. With the shoebox under one arm, she opened the door, walked in, and headed straight for the computer cubby. There, she was able to search for information on this little frog, and the best way to care for him. She keyed "care of frogs" into the search box. *Who would have thought there would be so many sites available on frogs and toads.* She thought to herself. As Anna found different information on what frogs ate and how their habitat should be made, she began to think that this was going to be a lot more work than Dino had planned for. Many frogs ate insects, but their habitats varied so much that she would need to know exactly what kind this one was. She looked at her watch and noticed that it was already getting late, and she had wanted to get to the forest. She tipped the lid of the shoebox up and peered in. There sitting in the bottom of the box was this tiny creature. Somehow, at that moment, his care seemed a bit more important than getting to the forest. "Well, little guy, let's take a look at you and see if we can figure you out." The little frog was only about an inch long, dark olive in color, with a lighter green stripe down his back. He had golden eyes and what looked like a dark green triangle pointed backward between his eyes. Anna gently picked up the tiny frog to get a closer look. He had slightly bumpy skin, and long hind legs with webbed toes. She carefully placed him back in his box and set the cover on leaving a small opening so she could look back at him. He backed into the dark corner of the box.

Anna began to type in the description of the frog. When she pressed enter, she could never have imagined what she was about to see. She read the first two sentences. "Huh," she gasped quietly. "Could this be right?" she read it again to herself; *The Blanchard's Cricket Frog is found in open edges of permanent ponds, bogs, lakes and slow-moving streams and rivers, in the Great Lakes Region. This frog was once common, but now has all but disappeared, and is considered an endangered species.*"

She tipped back the corner of the box and peeked in. "You, my little friend, are the answer to my prayers." Anna quickly looked up Blanchard's Cricket Frog and pressed image search. There he was, right on the screen in front of her. Then she searched what they ate: tiny insects, beetles, spiders, midge larvae, small slugs, and crickets.

Oh yuck, I guess table scraps are out for you, she thought. Suddenly, she heard a high pitched, "gick-gick-gick," sound. "Is that you?" she asked, looking at the box. She looked back at the page she was reading and noticed a link near the bottom, to hear its call. Anna took a deep breath and clicked the link. She leaned into the speaker and listened. It was the same call coming from the speaker that had come from the box. Anna looked around and saw the librarian standing behind the desk. She dropped the lid securely on the box and went to the desk.

"I'd like to print some pages from the computer over there," she said, pointing at the cubby she was sitting at.

"Ok, go ahead and hit print on the computer. It will print back here and you can pick them up before you leave. It is ten cents per page," replied the librarian.

"Great, thanks!" Anna said, and she hurried back to the cubby and started printing what she had found.

Chapter 29
Gone Missing

Karia woke early the following morning. She hadn't noticed that her little friend had jumped into the circle as Dino left. She thought it odd that he was not there, but she figured he just wandered off. "Maybe he went back home, too bad." Karia thought aloud. "I do miss him. Well, I should prepare to go to see Juna, Mim and Sire Argus." Karia went to Para and requested a turkey and a wagon. "I will be going to see my family on this day. I will not return until late tomorrow. Please let Oracle Balstar know," Karia told Para.

"I do believe he would much rather you take Arbalest Bendbow with you on such a long journey. It can be quite treacherous out there alone," Para replied, in a pleading tone.

"Well, I suppose it couldn't hurt. I am sure Sire Argus would enjoy the visit," Karia said, remembering her last trek home by herself.

"Very well, I shall summon Arbalest. He should be here by the time you are ready to set out," Para replied.

"Oh and by the way you haven't seen a little frog wandering around, have you?" Karia asked.

"No, dear, I have not," Para said, puzzled.

"That's OK! Maybe he stayed in the garden at the willow," Karia said, sounding thoughtful.

A short while later, there was a knock at the door to Karia's room. It was Arbalest, all ready for their journey.

"Well, that was quick," Karia stated, as she opened the door.

"Well, I thought I should get here before you decided to leave without me." He picked up Karia's bags, brought them to the wagon, and tossed them into the back. "Are you ready? It is a long journey! We should leave now if we wish to be there before nightfall."

Karia came out from behind the roots of the tree. "I am ready."

Para also met them at the wagon carrying a satchel. "These are so you won't be too hungry. There is plenty for the both of you." She handed the satchel to Karia after she was seated in the wagon.

Arbalest snapped the reins and the turkey pulled with a frightened jerk, as if he had been standing there asleep. The wagon pulled away through Mazus Grove. The vendors at the market were all packing up their wagons, as the sun had already begun to glow just below the horizon. Karia watched the other Traegons and wondered what there life would be like if they had to leave this place. *Where would we all go?* she thought sadly.

As they pulled toward the bog and the Royal Fern field, she thought of her little friend again. Karia began to scour the area as they continued on. She hoped she might see or hear her little friend and know he was all right. *I wonder if this is how Mim feels when we are not with her.* Karia wondered. She couldn't wait to see them. She settled back in her seat and watched the woods go by.

Dino C. Crisanti

Village Of Traegonia

Chapter 30
Building a Case

Anna hurried home and pulled out her camera from the buffet cabinet. She placed the box on the dining room table and removed the lid. The little frog was sitting patiently in the bottom of the box. Anna placed a large brown towel on the table with a glass casserole dish filled with water. She set an upside down brown shallow dish in the corner. She carefully removed the frog from the box and placed him on the makeshift island. The tiny frog sat very still and then crept forward and slipped into the water. He stayed in the water for quite a while. Anna used this time to set her camera to photograph him. Once she had her camera ready, she took the frog out and set him back onto the upside down dish. She was happy that he was so calm. She picked up her camera, set the flash and focused the lens. She snapped the first picture and the flash lit up the dish. The little frog didn't seem to like this because he leaped from the dish and landed in the middle of the dining table.

"Ohh, I am sorry, little one. Did that scare you?" Anna said, moving slowly toward the frog. She set down the camera and looked closely at the small and fragile creature. She reached her hand over to touch him with the tip of her finger. The little frog tucked his head in and hunched his back, turning himself into a little ball.

"Awe, you sure don't like the flash do you?" Anna picked up her camera again, shut off the flash, and began snapping more pictures. The frog sat still while she took several more pictures. Once she felt like she had gotten enough shots, she put him back into the box. She scooped some of the water into the shallow dish and placed the dish into the box. She slipped the lid back onto the box, wound the film and removed it from the camera. She picked up her purse, and went to leave, heading to the store to get the pictures developed. "I'll stop at the pet shop and get you some dinner while I'm out," Anna called back as she walked out.

She had an hour before the pictures would be ready, so she thought she would go and visit the lady from the DNR. The Department of Natural Resources office was only about fifteen minutes out of town. Anna pulled open the door to the DNR office and stepped in. The heavy wooden door clicked shut loudly behind her. There was no one sitting at the desk. She looked around at the signs and posters papering the walls. Fishing laws, hunting laws, information seminars, and maps filled the room. A moment later, a woman walked out from behind a wall carrying some papers.

"Oh, hello! How are you? Is there something I can help you with?" the woman greeted Anna.

"Yes, I called the other day asking for information on endangered species in the area?" Anna said.

"Yes, of course. I was just working on the information you requested.

I didn't expect you in so soon. I don't have it all complete just yet," the woman said, sitting down behind the desk. "What is it that I can help you with today?"

"I'm sorry, I don't remember your name. I'm Anna."

"My name is Pat," the woman behind the desk answered.

"Is it possible for you to give me information about a specific animal?" Anna asked, stepping closer to the desk.

"Well, I can certainly try. What do you have?" Pat pushed some papers aside and pulled out the keyboard to her computer.

"What can you tell me about the Blanchard Cricket frog?"

Anna leaned forward as Pat started typing on the keyboard. Pat sat reading and then answered.

"Well, you sure picked a tough one to start with. These are definitely endangered, but more than that, they have not been seen in this area in about ten years. They are not only on the endangered list, but they are now considered extinct. You would be much better off looking for something that is considered protected. You might just be wasting your time looking for something that may not even exist here anymore," Pat told Anna.

"What exactly would happen if I ran across something that was thought to be extinct?" Anna questioned cautiously.

"Well, we would need proof, of course. We would need to know where exactly they were living, pictures or some other documentation, something to prove your claims. Then I would put you in contact with the head of our conservation department. His name is Jake Avers. He would be able to help you," Pat informed my mother. "Do you want his name and phone number?"

"Yes, why don't you give me his information and I will just hold on to it for now," Anna stated. "Thank you for all of your help."

Anna took the information that Pat had written on the back of one of their cards. She smiled and told Pat that she would be back in a day or so to pick up the other information she was preparing.

"Good luck, Anna. I hope you find what you are looking for. Let me know if I can be of any more help."

"Thank you so much, you're very kind," Anna told her, smiling. "I definitely will." And the door closed hard behind her.

Anna drove back into town and stopped at the local pet shop. She picked out a small plastic reptile cage and a rock that would make a nice island inside. Then she approached a man to find out what type of food they carried for frogs. He showed her a few different options; some alive and some not. She bought a couple of them because she wasn't sure what he would actually eat. Then she went back to the car and headed to the store to pick up her pictures.

I walked into the kitchen after school and saw my mom sitting at the table flipping through some pictures.

"Hi Mom! I'm home!" I went to the refrigerator to get a glass of juice. "What are you looking at?"

Mom looked up. "You are never going to believe this. You know that little frog you brought home?"

"Yeah?" I answered.

"Well, it's an extinct species," she said, smiling.

"What? Are you kidding me?" I asked in disbelief. She placed the pictures and the printouts from the library on the table in front of me. I looked at the pictures she had taken and then looked at the picture on the printout. I looked at my mom. She was staring at me with a big smile on her face.

"Well, what do you think?" Mom asked me.

"It sure looks the same to me," I said. "Now what? Does this mean that we are going to be able to save the land?"

"I don't know for sure, but I think this is probably a really good sign. We still need to prove that this is the frog we think it is. I want to talk to your father before I mention it to anyone," Mom said, taking a sip of her coffee. "You will need to show me exactly you were when you found him."

My heart sank. What was I going to tell her? I really had no idea where these frogs were living. I had to talk to Karia, and soon. *How can I reach her?* my mind raced.

"Do you remember where you were?" Mom asked. "I am going to have to see when I get there. I walked around looking for you so it really could have been anywhere," I responded hoping we would be able to figure out exactly where he came from. "Where is he?" I asked, pushing away from the table.

"He's on the dining table," my mom answered.

I walked into the dining room. I saw the new home my mom had put together for him. "Mom, this is a great little house for him. Thanks for doing this for me."

"Well, I just thought he needed something better than a shoe-box," she answered from the kitchen.

I picked up the plastic box. "I am going upstairs to start on my homework." I announced as I grabbed my backpack and headed upstairs. I tossed my backpack on my bed and set the frog on my desk. I sat down and looked at him for a few minutes, thinking about how I could get a hold of Karia. Suddenly, I had a thought. I went over to my bed and pulled the box out from under the bed. I placed it on my desk and carefully opened it. The two items Karia had given me sat in the box. I took out the crystal and held it in my hand. I rolled it in my fingers and looked at the sunbow. I set it down on the desk and picked up the white acorn. I remembered that each time I had seen Karia, it was through the use of the acorn. "I wonder if I can use this to contact her?" I thought aloud. "Well, it can't hurt to try."

I held the acorn in the palm of my hand and wrapped my other hand over it. I closed my eyes tight and tried to see Karia in my mind. "Karia, I really need to talk to you. I hope you can hear me. It's really important. Karia! Karia! Can you hear me?" I repeated this over and over until I heard the back door. My dad was home. I opened my eyes and my hand. I had been holding the acorn so tight, it was hot to the touch. I placed it back into the box. Just then, my mom called for me to bring the frog downstairs to the kitchen. I left the box on my desk and picked up the frog and took him downstairs.

I walked into the kitchen and saw my dad looking through the pictures. "Hi, Dino!" he said. "Let me see this little guy."

I set the frog on the table. Dad pulled the box close to him and peered through the side. He looked back at the papers Mom had gotten from the library.

"Well, do you think it is really the same?" I asked.

"He sure does look like the same frog. Where did you say you found him?" He looked back at me.

"I don't really know exactly where, Dad. I was kind of all over.

I was looking for Mom. I stopped a couple of times and set my backpack down. I didn't notice him until after I got home."

"Well, I think we will have to try and figure it out. I will call Charlie at the forest preserve tomorrow," my father said.

"And I'm going to call Jake Avers from the conservation department at the DNR," Mom added.

"Sounds like a plan, all we can do now is cross our fingers and hope for the best. So what's for dinner?" Dad asked.

Chapter 31
Surprise Visit

Karia and Arbalest arrived at Karia's home before dark. Juna must have heard them pull up because he was at the door even before they were out of the wagon. Karia could hear him call Mim and Sire Argus. Mim and Sire Argus came out of their tree home.

"Oh, what a wonderful surprise!" Mim's voice was filled with so much joy. She ran up to Karia and hugged her tight. Sire Argus and Arbalest greeted one another. Sire Argus hugged Karia, and then helped Arbalest get the bags from the back of the wagon.

"Come in! Dinner is just about ready," Mim said, as she pulled Karia toward the door.

Karia went to her old room and began to take a few things from her bag. Juna sat in their room with her, and they reminisced about their trip to the house, and the pie. Karia removed her pouch. She had a sense that something was strange. She opened the pouch and dumped out the contents on her sleeping mat. She noticed that the dolphin charm that Dino had given her looked somehow different. She picked it up and looked closely at it. "What is it?" asked Juna.

"I am not sure," said Karia. "Something just seems odd. I do not know what it is." She looked at the charm again. It popped out of her hand and landed on the bed. "Did you see that?" she asked Juna.

"What do you think it means?" Juna responded.

"I have a feeling that Dino needs me. But I have never contacted him on my own. I have always summoned him at the willow with Oracle Balstar," Karia said. "I think I should try and reach him. But I will need your help. I have always had someone standing by. I will need you to do that for me. Should something go wrong, you will have to get word to Oracle Balstar. Do you understand?"

"Yes, I will do what you need me to do," Juna said.

"Ok, directly following our evening meal, we will tell Mim and Sire Argus that we want to spend some time together, and we will come back here and I will try to reach him."

As soon as they finished their meal and helped Mim clean up, they returned to their room. With the door shut, Karia sat on the floor and closed her eyes. She did not have the sacred circle or the burning cedar. She did not have Oracle Balstar or the power of the crystals and the solitude of the willow. But she did have determination, and a true connection with Dino.

Karia began to breathe deeply. She focused on her heartbeat. Bum, bum... bum, bum... bum, bum. Karia slowly began to feel herself being pulled backward. Back further and further with every beat of her heart. And then she fell through time and space, landing in the middle of Dino's room, waking him as she landed.

"Karia, I am so glad you are here! I've been trying to call you with my mind. I really didn't think it was going to work," I told her.

"I am a bit amazed myself. I am visiting Mim and Sire Argus and attempted this for the first time on my own. What did you need? Is there something wrong?" Karia asked.

"Nothing is wrong. I actually have great news. I just need your help. You know your little frog friend?" I asked Karia.

"Yes, but he went missing after the last time we saw each other," Karia responded.

"He's not missing. He returned with me. I planned to bring him to the forest with me this weekend, but my mother wanted to find out how to take care of him, and found out that he is an extinct species. He is exactly what we have been searching for. The only thing is, now we have to show others where he lives, and hopefully find more like him and then we can possibly save the land. This is huge, Karia. We are actually going to make this happen, you know, the prophecy."

Karia stood completely still listening to every word I said. "Dino, this is amazing! The only problem is that I have only seen one frog like this one, and when I found him, he was very near the heart of Traegonia."

"That is what I need you to find out. I need you to find out where they live, if there are more of them. Some people are going to have to come to where they are living. They will need to be sure that they are there so that they can approve the land to be protected, and his kind to be protected too. Do you think that you can do this, Karia?"

"Yes, Dino, but I will need to take him back with me. I will need to show others what he looks like, so that we can search for more of his kind," stated Karia.

"My mom will not understand if he is gone. What will I tell her?" I explained, with concern in my voice.

"Where is he, Dino?" Karia asked.

"He's over there on my desk." I pointed.

Karia walked across the room and climbed up the chair. She climbed onto the desk and looked into the plastic container. The little frog moved from the corner of the box and looked at Karia.

"I need to take him with me," Karia said again. She looked at Dino. "Tell your mother that you were looking at him and you accidentally left the lid off. Tell her you will look for him and promise you will find him. It will only be one day. I will bring him back to Oracle Balstar and we can call a community meeting. Everyone will see him and we can begin to search. I will return him to you tomorrow, about the same time."

I looked at Karia and then at the frog. "You know, Karia, my mom is going to have a fit. She is going to be so angry with me. She may never forgive me."

"Dino, I can fully understand your concern and if there was another way... but as far as we know, right now, he is the only one. Maybe he can somehow lead us to others. Please understand, I would never betray you and would never want to create a space between you and your mother. Maybe someday, just maybe, you will be able to share the truth. Please remove the lid, I have to be getting back now."

I reluctantly opened the plastic box. Karia called to the frog and he easily jumped out and landed in Karia's hands. She placed him on the desk and climbed down herself. The frog followed obediently. Karia walked to the center of the room and turned around. She looked up at me. The frog sat patiently at her side.

"I am sorry, Dino. Please know I wish you no harm. I will return him as quickly as I can."

Karia sat down on the floor and placed the frog in her lap. She closed her eyes and began to breathe deeply. In a few moments, she and the frog disappeared.

Karia appeared in the room where Juna had been keeping watch. There in her lap was the frog. She had forgotten that Juna had never seen her little friend.

"Where did you get him?" Juna asked almost immediately. "I thought you were going to see Dino."

"I did," said Karia. "Come with me. We have to show Mim, Sire Argus, and Arbalest." They went into the other room with the frog in tow. They were all surprised to see Karia and Juna come out of their room with a frog. Karia proceeded to share the story of the little frog and the important part he was to play in saving Traegonia. Everyone understood how important finding more of these creatures was.

"I am afraid we will have to cut our visit short. It is imperative that we return to Traegonia and inform the others of what has transpired. I hope you all understand. I promised Dino I would return this frog to him tomorrow. Please look closely at him, and I ask that you all look for more of them. They will be found near water."

The little frog interrupted with his unique gick, gick call. "And this is what he sounds like," Karia added. They all laughed.

"We had better retire as we should set off on our journey back as early as possible," stated Arbalest Bendbow.

"Yes, you are correct. We should probably leave well before sunrise," Karia added.

"Well then, goodnight, my young. Sleep well," Mim said, kissing both Karia and Juna. "It is wonderful to have both my younglings within our home again, if only for one night."

Karia and Juna went back into their room and the little frog followed. Karia and Juna each lay down on their sleeping mats, dimmed their lantern, and closed their eyes. Karia felt the urge to open her eyes and when she did, she was looking sideways into the face of the little frog. She lay there for a moment and then propped herself up on one elbow. She looked deep into the little frog's golden eyes. Juna had fallen asleep so Karia thought in her mind, *Do you understand all that is going on, little frog? I need to know where you are from and if there are more like you. It is very important and we will make sure that you will not be harmed.*

The little frog tilted his head and continued to stare at Karia. She waited a few moments and then smiled. "Get some sleep, little one," she said to the frog, and then lay back on her sleeping mat. Suddenly, the words poured into her head. It reminded her of when Sable guided her home. This is what she heard: *"There are a few clans of us. We live separate but near enough. I wandered off chasing a fly and lost my way. I called but I only found you."*

Karia opened her eyes and turned her head, the little frog was still sitting next to her, staring at her.

The words continued. *"If you help me find my clan, then I am sure we can help you."*

Karia blinked. *Are you talking to me?* She asked with her thoughts.

Gick, gick, was the response. Karia smiled and went to sleep.

Chapter 32
Disappointing Mom

I woke up the next morning. I hadn't slept well at all. I was tossing and turning, worrying about what I was going to tell my mother. I lay awake for a long time, when I heard the call I was dreading.

"Dino, it's time to get up for school," she called from the bottom of the stairs.

I pulled the covers over my head and wished Karia had not taken the frog with her. "Dino, did you hear me? Are you awake, up there?" she called again.

I knew I had to answer. "I'm up, Mom! I'll be down in a little while," I hollered back.

"Bring that little friend of yours with you when you come," she chimed back, sounding like she was in a very good mood.

My stomach sank. I had such a knot in it and it was getting worse. Now I was going to absolutely destroy her day. All wanted to do was tell her the truth, but I just couldn't go back on the promise I made to Karia either. I got dressed thinking about what I was going to do, what would I tell her to make it easier on her. I began to just pretend in my own mind that Karia and I hadn't met last night. I walked over to the desk where the little plastic frog house sat. I looked at it and saw the lid leaning up against the side. I gasped.

"MOM! MOM! Come up here. MOM! Hurry!" I could hear her

running up the stairs and then my door burst open. "Dino, what's going on? What's wrong?"

I looked at her and then back at the cage. She looked too, and then walked slowly over to the desk. She was silent. When she got to the desk, she bent over and looked closely into the plastic cage. Then she stood and looked at me. In a quiet puzzled tone, she said, "What happened, Dino? Where is the frog?"

I took a step back. "I... I don't know. I was looking at him last night before I went to sleep, and I guess I must have left the lid off. When I got up this morning, he was gone." I paused looking at her for a reaction. "I looked all over, Mom, I don't see him anywhere. I'm really sorry, Mom."

My mom looked carefully at the floor and pulled out the desk chair. She slowly sat down and scanned the floor of my room. She looked me directly in the eyes and in a very calm and monotone voice, she began to speak. "Do you have any idea what you have done? This may have been our only chance to save this land. How could you be so careless?" I could hear anger building in her voice. I took another step back. "As concerned, respectful individuals, I feel it is our responsibility to care for the land and the creatures that inhabit it. I thought we had taught you these values as well." She looked away.

"You did, Mom... you did," I pleaded, taking a tentative step toward her.

She looked back with tears in her eyes. "I love you, Dino, but I am so disappointed in you right now that I just have to leave this room before I say something I may regret later." She stood up and walked toward the door.

"He'll turn up, Mom. I will search the house top to bottom when I get home from school." She stepped through the doorway. "Mom, I promise we'll find him," I said, as she pulled the door closed behind her. I let out a huge sigh and collapsed on my bed. *That went well,* I thought sarcastically. *I think I'll go throw up now.* I picked up my things and sneaked out the front door. I couldn't bear to see my mom, and I didn't think she really wanted to see me right now either.

Chapter 33
Help From a Most Unlikely Place

Karia and Arbalest returned to the willow early the next day. The green-eyed dragonfly announced our coming and purpose with a message from Mim. The community was summoned to a gathering just outside the willow. When Karia and Arbalest pulled their wagon into the clearing just beyond Mazus Grove, they saw a large crowd of Traegons assembled near the willow. They also saw Bayalthazar soaring through the sky with another Unpuzzlier in his new flying machine. As they got closer, they could see Oracle Balstar, Master Zoal, and the elders gathered outside as well.

"Welcome back! We are excited to see your friend and begin our search," Sir Antar stated with a kind and excited tone in his voice.

Karia was stunned at how much information they already had. Arbalest stopped the wagon and told Karia to climb into the back to address the community. She climbed into the back and stacked a couple of bags on top of each other, next to her. The little frog jumped onto the makeshift pedestal. Karia looked at Oracle Balstar; he nodded once for her to proceed. "Fellow Traegons," Karia began, "I stand before you and ask for your assistance in a very important matter. This little frog is one of only a small group left in our land. It is very important that we find his kind within the boundaries of Traegonia. We ask that each of you spend some time searching near any water areas within our borders. Do not remove them from their homes. Only return with the information as to where we might find them. This will not be an easy task, but we must find them rather quickly. Please form a line and view this little frog well. We are only looking for his kind, not other common frogs from our areas."

"What is the purpose of this?" a voice piped up from the crowd.

Karia looked to Oracle Balstar. She knew that the community had not been given full details of the Sunbow Prophecy coming to fruition. Oracle Balstar climbed up onto the wagon and addressed the crowd.

"You have all been made aware of the Sunbow Prophecy and that Karia has been working with myself and the elders to determine if this is the time that the prophecy is to be realized. We have come to the conclusion that the prophecy is unfolding at this time."

First a gasp came from the crowd, and then a low hum of chatter quickly spread through the crowd. Oracle Balstar tapped his cane loudly on the wagon. The group quieted.

"We have been working steadily to gain full and accurate information before addressing the community. Now we need your help. We have always worked to keep Traegonia safe, and we continue to do so. Now, I will hold a community meeting this day, directly at midday to communicate the full details and share all of the information we have acquired, as it is now time. As for this moment, you are asked to view this creature, no matter how small and insignificant it may seem to you, it is important to Traegonia and our survival. Divide into groups and find these creatures. We have always come together to help one another in times of need. This is one of those times."

Oracle Balstar turned and climbed off of the wagon. A line of Traegons' began to file past the wagon, looking closely at the little frog, who sat contently. It took a while for everyone to view the little frog. Once they had all seen him, groups could be seen gathering to make their own plans to begin the search. Oracle Balstar approached the wagon.

"Karia," he began, "you and your little friend may return to your room, Para has a meal waiting there for you. You are not required to attend the meeting as I understand you have work of your own to do before returning the frog to Dino. Arbalest will go with you to attempt to locate the little frog's family."

Everyone returned to their own work, and Karia and the little frog met Para for their meal.

Later that afternoon, Karia, Arbalest, and the little frog met in Mazus Grove. They returned to the place where Karia had first met her small friend. She sat on the ground directly in front of the little frog and looked deep into his golden eyes. She asked, "What do you remember about your home? Can you remember what direction you came from, or if you moved through grass, leaves, water, or mud before you found yourself here?"

The little frog sat quietly. He looked around a bit and then returned his gaze to Karia. *"It is hard for me to recall. I was not attending to where I was going, or I would not have found myself lost. My home is beside the water, small water, not like the great river. But I know of the river because it feeds our small water home. There is tall grass and a field of cattails that tower over our home. Does this help?"*

Karia shared what the frog had told her with Arbalest. He suggested that they go to the river, from the closest point to where they were and then follow the river to the creeks that off shoot the river.

Once they reached the river, the little frog looked up and down the river, as did Karia and Arbalest. *"I followed the fly against the current,"* Karia heard in her mind. She looked at the frog and he began to hop downstream. Karia and Arbalest followed close behind. Arbalest saw a tree up ahead and went before them. He climbed up and looked around. "I see a cluster of cattails ahead and off to the left. We will check there first." They continued on and soon came to a small stream that broke off from the river. The little frog chirped his very unique sound. Gick, gick, gick. Gick, gick, gick. He chirped again. They moved through the dense brush along the stream.

"Shh," Karia stopped. "Listen." They were very quiet. Suddenly, they heard a very faint gick, gick ......gick, gick. The little frog became excited as he recognized the sound of his clan. He called back, gick, gick, gick... Karia and Arbalest had to move quickly to keep up. As the little frog slowed his jumps, Karia and Arbalest slowed their strides. They noticed several dark popping figures in the distance, but as they moved closer, everything was still. They were able to see the little frog sitting at the edge of the stream in a muddied clearing bordered by some green growth. Arbalest and Karia stood very still, watching for movement. Moments later, they saw four frogs crawl out from a hidden home. Karia stepped forward slowly and knelt down on one knee. She felt very large over them. In her thoughts, she could hear the little frog persuade the others to come out and not to be afraid. She heard him explain to the others of the quest for their kind, for the purpose of saving this land, and their home as well. The four little frogs looked up at Karia. Karia spoke out loud.

"This is all true. The humans have stated that your kind have not been seen in these parts for many moons. We would be very grateful if you would allow yourselves to be seen by a few humans. We promise to be close and protect you if needed." Karia waited for a response.

"*We will help,*" she heard in her thoughts, followed by them chirping all together.

"My little friend, I still need you to stay with me a bit longer. Remember, Dino needs to show you to others. It is my understanding that he will return you here in a day or two," Karia reminded her little friend.

"*Will you be able to find this place again?*" requested the little frog through Karia's thoughts. Karia looked to Arbalest and repeated the question.

"I will be able to find and lead Dino to this place. I know exactly where we are," Arbalest reassured all of them.

"Very well, we should circle back to the willow and await our return to Dino on this eve. All is going perfectly. As Mim always says, 'When it is to be, the Universe guides our way.' We must go now, we will bring him home soon. Oh, and please remember, if you see or hear the humans near, make your calls so that they can find you. We are all grateful for your assistance in this matter."

Karia stood. "Come now, little friend," she said to the small frog. The three moved through the dense woods back toward the river and onto the willow.

Chapter 34
Frog's Return

I came home from school that afternoon and reluctantly came through the back door. No one was home. I was relieved but also wondered where everyone was. I went straight to my room, hoping to see the little frog back in his plastic container, but I was disappointed to see it still empty. I sat down to do my homework and a little while later I heard the back door. Someone was home. I walked to the top of the stairs and listened. I heard both my parents' voices coming from the kitchen. I slowly walked down the stairs and listened. "I talked to Charlie at the Forestry Division and showed him the picture you gave me," my dad said.

"And?" asked my mom.

"Well, he was very interested in the picture and said that if we can show him where these frogs are now living, he will go before the board and formally request the land to be designated a protected site," said Dad.

"That's wonderful, Jack," my mom responded in a very excited tone.

"Well, hold on. He did say that on certain occasions, they will just relocate the animal, which would leave the land open for private sale," my dad told her.

"You know, Jack, I have been thinking," Mom paused. "Why don't we buy the house?"

Dad looked at my mother, puzzled. "Anna, we can't afford to buy all of that land. And we have a house right here."

"I know, I'm not talking about buying all of the land, just the house and a couple of acres," Mom responded calmly. "This is a lovely house, but it is almost paid off and we always wanted to live in a more secluded, wooded area. Plus, it is still in Dino's school district, so he could still go to the same school. Just think about it. Anyway, I went back to the DNR today and showed the pictures to the woman there. She was really impressed and a bit stunned. She contacted Jake Avers from the conservation department, and he was very intrigued. He wants to see the frog and where it was found."

"So, Anna, how do you intend to pull that off, since your son lost the frog and can't even remember where he found it?" Dad asked sarcastically.

Mom shot my dad a look. "Jack, I know he didn't mean to leave the top off. He promised to look through his room and the whole house today after school."

Just then, I poked my head around the corner. "Hi!" I said sheepishly.

"Oh, hi Dino. How long have you been home?" Mom asked.

"Just a little while," I responded. "I heard what you said."

"All of it?" asked my father.

"Yeah, can we really buy that house? It is such a nice place and it's surrounded by forest on all sides."

"How do you know so much about the house? When were you there?" my father asked.

I realized that they were not aware of my visit with Mr. Rhodes. "Well, that day when I told you I went by the forest and couldn't find Mom, I thought I would just ride my bike down the road a bit and take a look. I walked through the trees all the way to the river." I tried to think fast.

"You cannot just walk onto someone else's property without permission. That is trespassing. You should know better. What were you thinking?" my father scolded.

"So it is very possible that you picked that little frog up on those people's land, and not at the public forest preserve," my mom said, as if devising a plan.

"Anna!" my dad snapped. "He was trespassing! That's illegal. Are you with me here?"

Mom had this look in her eye. "Yes, yes, I'm with you. Dino, you must ask permission before you go onto someone else's property. Do you think you can remember exactly where you went? Where you might have picked up the frog?"

My dad shot my mother an annoyed look, but she didn't seem to notice. She just stared at me, waiting for my answer.

"Um, well, I might be able to remember if I see it again," I replied, without having a clue.

"Well, I need you to go upstairs and search your room top to bottom for that little frog. I think what we should plan to do is have your friend Charlie from the forestry department and Jake Avers from the conservation department with the people from DNR meet us at the man's home on Saturday, and Dino can show them where he was on that day. We can try and talk to the owner of the house at the same time. We just might be able to head off this developer before he has a chance to sink his teeth in. This is so great! Everything is working out so well!" Mom announced.

After dinner, I went to my room and worked on my homework, and did some drawing in my journal. I kept hoping and wondering if Karia would bring the frog back and if she didn't what was I was going to tell my parents. The evening lingered on with no sign of Karia.

"Dino! Dino! Wake up!" Karia's voice broke into my sleep. I opened my eyes and gratefully saw Karia standing over me. "I don't have much time but I have a lot to tell you," she whispered.

I sat up in my bed and looked at her as I tried to wake up. The little frog hopped up on my bed and sat attentively next to her.

"Listen carefully to me. Take whoever it is you need to show the frog's existence to into the woods the day after next. It is closer if you enter the woods through the elderly man's land. Arbalest and I will be nearby to guide you to the place. You will not see us. Listen for this sound. She made a bird sound that I hadn't heard before. "Can you remember this?"

"Yes, I can remember," I replied.

"The frog will remain with you until then," she continued. "You will need to return him to his home when you get there. As you get close, the frog will chirp. This will tell you that you are near. Listen, as his clan will respond. They will lead you in. You must take care and move slowly. They will allow themselves to be seen, but you and the others will not, and cannot attempt to catch them. This is a promise we have made. They are willing to help us, but only with the promise that they will remain safe. You must return this frog. Do you understand?" Karia looked directly into my eyes with an intense seriousness I hadn't seen before.

"I understand completely," I answered

"Very good, I must go now. I will see you soon." Karia grabbed the comforter on my bed and slid to the floor. She went to the middle of the room, closed her eyes, and disappeared. I picked up the frog and placed him in the plastic cage and clicked the top back on. I returned to bed and fell asleep.

Chapter 35
The Confirmation

I woke early, jumped out of bed, and hurried to my desk. There was the little frog sitting contently. I breathed a sigh of relief and muttered under my breath, "He's back." Then I bolted out of my room and down the stairs. I slid around the corner and into the kitchen, where my mother was sitting drinking her coffee.

"He's back! He's back!" I shouted with an excitement I didn't have to act.

"What? Did you find him?" My mom asked, moving to the edge of her seat.

"I looked all last night. I called to him like he was a dog or something, I looked under my bed, in the closet, down the hall, even in the bathroom, but I couldn't find him anywhere. Then when I woke up this morning, he was just sitting there in the cage." I took a deep breath.

"Are you serious? He went back in his cage by himself?" Mom, asked, amazed.

"Maybe he needed some water or maybe he got hungry or something," I responded.

She stood and headed up the stairs. I guess she just needed to see it for herself.

"Unbelievable," she whispered. "Well, let's get moving. It's going to be a busy day. Get ready for school. I'm going to hop in the shower. I have some people to see about a frog and some land." She smiled and walked out.

This was actually pretty exciting. All we had worked for and hoped for felt like it was really going to work out.

Saturday came fast. I had been replaying the conversation I had had with Karia in my head over and over again. This was going to be a really important day, and could probably determine the outcome for everything. Mom and Dad were busy the day before trying to get all of the important people together for this meeting, which wasn't real hard considering the live discovery of an extinct creature was of interest to many of them. If the land wasn't very important, this was. Mom made an appointment to meet these people at the elderly man's house after lunch. We were going early so that my mom and dad could introduce themselves and get permission to be on the property. I was a little nervous, but I knew we had to do this.

We left our house with the frog, and got to Mr. Rhodes house around 10:45 a.m. We all got out of the car and walked up to the front door. I could see my mother looking around the property and at the house. I knew she was still thinking about buying it, but I didn't think my dad was real excited about the idea. I stood behind my parents. I still hadn't told them I had met Mr. Rhodes before. My dad reached out and knocked on the wooden screen door. The door squeaked open and Mr. Rhodes stood in the doorway with a grumpy look on his face.

"Hi Mr. ...?" My mother paused so he could fill in the blank.

"Rhodes, my name is Jim Rhodes. Whatever you're selling, I don't want any," he grumbled.

"Oh, Mr. Rhodes, we're not here to sell you anything. My name is Anna Dosek, and this is my husband, Jack, and this is my son, Dino." She stepped to the side revealing me hiding behind her. Mr. Rhodes squinted his eyes and looked down at me. I smiled, waved a shy little wave, and looked at him in a way as to say, "Please don't know me." I know he recognized me but he didn't say anything to give me away.

"Okay, so what is this about?" Mr. Rhodes grumbled again.

"Well, Mr. Rhodes, we are aware that you are in negotiations on a possible deal to sell your property, and we are a bit concerned."

"How is my business any of your concern?" Mr. Rhodes said, sounding more annoyed than ever. I could tell my dad wasn't pleased with the way he was talking to my mom.

"Mr. Rhodes, we mean you no harm and we are sorry for any inconvenience we have caused. We would just like to talk with you for a few minutes," my dad stated in a kind but stern tone.

Mr. Rhodes looked at me and then back at my dad. "Oh, alright! Go on."

My mother continued, "Mr. Rhodes, we frequent the forest preserve that borders your property and have admired your land for years. Your property is an important part of the landscape of this town, and when we heard the man interested in buying it only wishes to tear it all down and build a shopping mall, well, it really disturbed me and my family. I wish we could purchase it ourselves, but it is much too much land for us to be able to afford. So we spoke to some people from the forestry department and the conservation department. They would also be sorry to see this land sold off for that purpose, but would be unable to obtain funding unless this land proved to hold something needing to be protected. So we have been trying to locate information on any species in this area that are officially protected."

Mr. Rhodes listened to my mother's words. He glanced over at me a few times.

Mom continued, "Now, Mr. Rhodes, my son, Dino, shared with me that he had come onto your property without your permission, which we scolded him for and explained the importance of always

asking permission first. But while he was on your land, he unknow-
ingly picked up a frog that belongs here."

Mr. Rhodes looked at me and again squinted his eyes. I smiled
sheepishly and said, "I didn't see him climb into my bag. I didn't even
notice him until I got home. But he is important," I said, holding up
the plastic container.

"Yes, he is very important," Mom added. "His species has actually
been considered extinct in this area for several years now. We have talked to the Forestry Department and the Department of Conservation,
as well as the Department of Natural Resources. They have all agreed
to meet us here today to see if we can locate their habitat."

"Okay, so let me get this straight," Mr. Rhodes cleared his throat
and continued, "if you find this frog living on my land, then my land
becomes protected, making it even harder to sell, since the land then
cannot be developed."

Our excitement was dwindling with his difficult attitude. Then
my dad spoke. "Mr. Rhodes, let me try to explain further. We are not
trying to hinder the sale of your property. We are trying to get the
land sold to people who would want to see it preserved for everyone
to enjoy. I am not going to ask you what the developer offered. I just
want you to hear what these men we are meeting with today have to
say. Ultimately, this is your land, and you have the right to do with
it what you want. We are just asking for permission to walk through
the woods on your property today. Is that fair enough?"

Mr. Rhodes took a deep breath. "Go, walk around all you want.
Just let me know what you find." He reached out his hands. "Let me
take a look at that critter you've got there."

I stepped up and handed the container over to Mr. Rhodes.
"Huh," he said looking through the plastic. "He's really a little guy. I
don't know how you figure on finding more like him. This is a lot of
land." He looked closer. "You say he is supposed to be extinct, huh?"
he asked, as he handed it back to me.

"Yes, sir, and that's why we've gotta help them, so they don't go away again," I said, with some urgency in my voice.

"Well, good luck. I suppose he deserves a place to live too." Mr. Rhodes looked at his watch. "Well, you had better get going. My daughter is coming to take me to lunch and I don't want to keep her waiting."

Mom and Dad shook hands with Mr. Rhodes and thanked him for his time. We all walked down the front steps and headed to the car. It wouldn't be long before the other's would be here. As we got near our car, another car approached. It was Sara, Mr. Rhodes' daughter. She looked confused to see people here, but smiled and waved anyway. We smiled and waved back. We got into our car and Dad pulled the car all the way over to the side of the yard near the woods. Moments later, a blue pickup truck, a brown car that said 'Conservation' on the side and a green SUV with DNR plates on it pulled up. They passed Sara and Mr. Rhodes on their way out.

The pickup and the brown car pulled up and parked behind our car. My mom and dad got out, and I followed, carrying the frog. Dad greeted his friend Charlie, who then introduced Jake Avers from the Department of Conservation, and Ron Anderson from the Department of Natural Resources. The lady my mom had met at the DNR office also came along.

"Hi, Pat!" my mom said. "So glad you could come, I didn't expect you to be here."

"Well, I couldn't pass up the opportunity to see an extinct species rediscovered in my own town. This is a really big deal if it's true," responded Pat with a smile.

I walked to the front of our car and set the container on the hood and stepped back. They all came in close to take a look. First, Jake Avers bent over and looked in, then picked up the container and held it up. He examined the frog for a long time and then set it back on the car. He picked up a manila folder and flipped through a few pages silently while Charlie, Ron, and Pat all took turns viewing the frog.

"From as near as I can tell, this *IS* a Blanchard Cricket Frog. And all my records indicate that this frog all but disappeared from this area around ten years ago. Do you know where you found it, young man?" Mr. Avers looked at me.

"Well, not exactly. I was here on the day I found him in my room. I think he must have climbed into my backpack," I responded. The man looked at me with a strange puzzled look. "I can take you where I was that day. I can show you where I set my backpack down." I tried to convince him that it was here, where I had found the frog.

"Okay, then, let's take a walk," he said.

We walked toward the back of the yard. I was in the lead so I felt like I was really being watched. I walked slowly, carefully looking around to see if I could find Karia but I didn't see her at all. I wasn't sure where I should enter the woods, so I just kept walking as if I knew where I was going. Suddenly, I heard a faint bird call it was the sound Karia had told me to listen for. It was coming from off to the left of the yard. I began to follow it. I found a narrow clearing that would have to do as a path. I pushed the tree branches back as I walked in. My mom followed me first, then my dad, and then the others. Every few minutes, I heard the call. I couldn't see Karia, but I knew she would take me where I needed to go. We walked for a long time. I began to hear the sound of the river. Then I heard my dad's voice.

"Dino, are you sure you know where you are going?" he asked, pushing through the dense woods.

"Sure I do," I answered, hoping I was right. Finally, I pushed through to a clearing at the edge of the river. I looked up and down the river, listening for my guide. "The bank is pretty narrow here, so be careful," I called back, as the rest of the group neared the river. Finally, I heard it. The call was faint, but I could tell it was coming from upstream. I turned and walked carefully along the riverbank.

"What were you doing so far out here?" my mom asked.

I thought quickly, for a moment. "When I didn't see you over at the picnic area, I thought I would ride along the road and see if I could see you through the woods. Then I ended up at that man's house, and figured I would go into the woods from there."

I looked over my shoulder at my mother. She was trying not to fall into the river, but looked at me with a certain look. I don't know if she believed me or not, but I thought as long as I stuck to my story, I would be okay. I slowed down a little and listened for Karia's call. I heard a sound but it wasn't Karia's call. I knew I had heard it before but I couldn't place it. As I started to move away from the riverbank and in the direction of the new sound, a gick, gick, came from the plastic container. *Oh, that's where I heard it before,* I thought as I giggled to myself. I stopped and turned to the others. "Listen." They all stopped and became very still and silent.

"We must be close. They're calling to each other." The others moved in close to me to try and listen. Then it happened again. A faint gick, gick, followed shortly by the frog in my hands calling back, gick, gick. Jake from the Conservation Department pushed past the others and came right up next to me.

"It's coming from over there," he said, pointing down a small stream that came off from the river. All I could see was a lot of tall grass. There really wasn't much room to walk back there.

"I don't think we should all try walking back there. I don't want to chance stepping on any of them," I said.

"Dino's right. Why don't you and Jake go? We can stay here," my mom agreed.

Jake pulled out a small camera from a pocket on the side of his pant leg, and began walking in the direction of the sound. He seemed excited as he pushed carefully through the dense brush and through the tall grasses.

"Shh," he said, coming to a stop. We listened closely and heard more gick, gick, sounds. They sounded as if they were right under our feet. I popped off the lid of the container with the frog in it.

"WAIT!" Jake snapped. I held the cover on tight.

"What? You almost made me drop the box," I said, annoyed.

"Sorry, kid! Just don't let him go yet. I need to get a couple of pictures," Jake said, moving close to where I was standing. Jake steadied his camera and then asked me to lift the lid slowly. I did as I was instructed and Jake took several pictures. We looked down along the small stream and noticed small black things popping several feet up the stream from us. Jake told me to stay there as he moved in very slowly and quietly. He bent down on one knee and crept forward. He quickly snapped a bunch of pictures.

"Okay, let him go down there, and let's see what he does." I opened the container and before I could put my hand in, the little frog jumped out. At first, I couldn't see where he went, but then he caught my eye as he made his way back to his home. Jake continued to snap pictures. Then he slowly stood and looked around.

"Amazing!" he said. "I had no idea how beautiful it was back here. Look," he said, pointing off in the distance, "See those dead trees. That is a perfect nesting place for the Common Barn Owl, which is also highly protected in our state. They are also an endangered species in this area."

Jake began to walk back to where I was. "Really? You think there could be more animals?" I asked. "Sure! It doesn't look like there has been anyone back here in a very long time. Let's get back and see what we can come up with." We all walked back through the woods and back to the cars. "I am extremely excited about this rediscovery of the Blanchard Cricket Frog. I will get copies of these pictures over to you by Monday, Pat. Then the DNR will also have a file on this. I will get you some as well, Charlie. I have a few ideas and people to call. I should have some concrete answers by the end of the week. Thank you, Anna, for bringing this to our attention, and you too,

Dino. You have no idea the impact this can have. Thank you again." Jake shook hands with everyone there, including me, and then got into his car and drove away. We all felt a sense of excitement and relief. My dad thanked Charlie, Ron, and Pat for coming out also.

"I guess we'll all be in touch sometime in the coming week," my dad said, and we all went our separate ways.

Chapter 36
Just Relax

Sunday morning, we got up and decided to go to the forest and relax. Things had been so tense the last few weeks, we just decided to "take a day", like my dad says. As soon as I got to the picnic area, I was off to the woods. I walked into the woods, excited to talk to Karia. I was just hoping she would be around. I was smiling and cheerful when suddenly someone grabbed me hard by the arm, and pulled me behind a mound of bushes. My heart was pounding when I was spun around and found myself face-to-face with Mr. Billson. "Look, kid! You and your family have been causing me a lot of grief. You need to tell your family to let this go if you know what's good for you," he growled.

"Let me go! Let me go!" I wiggled and hollered.

"Shut up, boy. You're going to take my message to your parents or else."

"Or else what? I'll take your message straight to the police, creepy old man in the woods, grabbing kids. They might want to hear about that." I somehow felt really brave. Then Mr. Billson raised his hand to hit me when something knocked him down. I looked around and saw nothing. I looked down at Mr. Billson and he was just getting up, which is when I thought it a good idea to run. He grabbed my leg and I fell down hard.

"HELP! HELP! HEEELP!" I hollered as loud as I could, as I tried to get away, then I heard a whoosh pass by my ear. When I looked back, Mr. Billson was sitting dumbfounded with a tiny arrow through his hat.

"What's going on here, boy? You got someone out here with you?"

"I sure do, but you wouldn't believe me anyway," I answered, looking around for Karia and Arbalest Bendbow. Then my mom and dad came fast up the path. "Let go of my son, Mr. Billson," my mom's voice sounded completely furious.

"Oh great, its y..." he almost finished, before my dad punched him hard in the jaw. My dad pulled me to my feet and grabbed my mom's hand. "If I catch you near my family again, you're going to find yourself behind bars," my dad growled, before we turned and walked off.

That wasn't the end for Mr. Billson that afternoon, as I found out later from Karia.

When we left, Mr. Billson heard a deep whisper from behind him. "We see you, we know what you are doing." Mr. Billson turned fast, but there was no one there.

"Who's there? Quit playing games," he yelled in an uneasy tone.

"The only one playing any games here is you, and you will not win. You will not win!" The deep whisper came again. This time, Billson felt warm breath on his neck. He scrambled to stand, crawling a few feet before he could bring himself to a running start, and then he was gone.

The run-in with Mr. Billson had cut our day short at the forest. My dad was so angry that he just wanted to go home. He told both my mom and me to stay away from the forest until the land issue was resolved. We weren't too happy about that.

"The forest is a public place and we shouldn't have to be run out just because Billson's plan isn't working out for him," my mom argued.

"I understand," my dad responded, "but who knows what he is capable of. If you see him around, or he approaches either of you again, I want the police called. Do you understand?"

My mom and I both agreed, mostly because when my father was that upset about something, there was no arguing with him. I was also angry at Mr. Billson. I had been really looking forward to seeing Karia today, and I was mad that now he made it so I didn't know when we might be going back to the woods. I was glad that they were there to help me, though. Even though I didn't see them, the small arrow was unmistakably Arbalests'.

We ate dinner early and just relaxed around the house. I drew in my journal and thought about Karia and Juna. I took out the crystal and the white acorn, and laid them on my desk. I stopped drawing long enough to try and communicate with Karia through my thoughts. I figured she had heard me once, why not a second time. I was hoping she would come tonight just so we could talk. It felt like it had been a long time since we had just spent time talking. I wanted to find out what was going on in Traegonia, and tell her how good things went on Saturday.

Chapter 37
Visit to Traegonia

Back in Traegonia, Karia and Arbalest were meeting with the other Traegons to gather more information on any other groups of frogs that they might have found in another areas of Traegonia. As they were going from one home to the next, Karia noticed a wagon coming into view. Moments later, she recognized it as Mim and Sire Argus' wagon and she began to run toward the wagon. Arbalest walked behind.

"What are you doing here?" Karia exclaimed as she got closer. Juna popped up from behind Sire Argus.

"Karia!" he yelled. The wagon slowed to a stop, and Karia excitedly hugged each one of them.

"What are you doing here?" she repeated.

"We have come to share information with the others and we thought we would stay the night and visit with you," Mim told her. Karia looked at Mim, and Mim at Karia and they both smiled. Karia and Arbalest hopped into the back of the wagon with Juna and Sire Argus continued toward the willow.

"What do you have to share?" Karia asked.

"Well, we have spent much time searching near our home for something sacred to the humans, and I think we may have come across something," Mim told her.

Sire Argus pulled the wagon up to the willow and a Sentinel immediately appeared to take the wagon. Moments later, Oracle Balstar appeared.

"Good day to you, my friends. Was the surprise as expected?" he said, looking at Karia.

"Oracle, you knew they were coming?" Karia asked Oracle Balstar.

"You have worked so hard for our community, I wanted to allow you a few days to spend with your family. I know, when you were home last you had to leave sooner than expected, at least when you are here, if you are needed, your family can stay and wait for you. Now, the Sentinel will show your family to their quarters."

Karia was so happy her family was there. Mim and Sire Argus went on to their room to unpack and rest after their trip. Karia took Juna out to show him around Traegonia. They walked and talked and laughed and reminisced. As they were out, Karia felt the same feeling she had when she had last visited home. She sensed that Dino needed her again. Because she didn't know if it was urgent or not, she planned to journey that evening when everyone had gone to sleep. Except this time, she wanted to try and take Juna with her.

That evening, Juna stayed with Karia in her room and as soon as the rest were asleep, she chose a place in the middle of the room. She sat down and motioned for Juna to sit next to her. She explained to him that he should hold her hand and not let go. She directed him to close his eyes, relax, and to breathe deeply, listening only to the beating of his heart. "Just hold on to my hand and do not let go. I have never tried this before and I am not sure if it will work, but if we do journey, I do not want to lose you in the process."

They both closed their eyes and held tight to each other's hand. Karia visualized a bright white light surrounding them both like a beautiful bubble. She knew the power of the white light and hoped and believed that this would protect them and keep them safe, and together. Breathing deeply and focusing only on the sound of their own breath, they both felt themselves being pulled backward with each beat of their hearts. This was not a new feeling for Karia but even though Juna felt very relaxed, he still had some fear of the unknown. Back, back, back until they both felt themselves falling and falling, then suddenly they landed with a thud. Karia's eyes popped open. She looked over at Juna. He was still sitting with his eyes closed tight.

"Juna," she whispered, "are you alright?"

Juna slowly opened one of his eyes and then both, he then looked at Karia. "Yes, I think so." He looked at himself to make sure he was all there. Then he looked around the room. "Are we here?" he asked.

Karia stood up and Juna followed. "Yes, we are here," she responded.

"Everything looks so large," Juna said, as the moonlight streamed through the window, allowing them plenty of light to see by. Karia started toward the bed across the room.

"Dino, Dino, wake up!" Karia whispered loudly.

I opened my eyes and listened, again I heard her calling me. I sat up and looked over the side of my bed. There they were, Karia and Juna both looking up at me. Excitedly I moved to help them up onto my bed.

"I am so glad you came," I told them both.

"Were you trying to contact me earlier?" Karia asked.

"I was. How did you know?" I asked her.

"I cannot be sure. I just get a sense of it. Is there something wrong?" asked Karia curiously.

"No, I just wanted to talk to you. You were in the woods today, weren't you?" I prodded.

"Yes, Arbalest and I were there. That man is a crazy one, I was worried for your safety. I am glad that Arbalest is such a good shot, as we did not wish to harm him, only scare him off of you." Karia blinked her eyes at me.

"I am glad you were there, too," I told them. "But I was also angry because we didn't have a chance to talk or just spend time together. The people who came to see the frog and where they live seemed excited about them. They said they would call us next week and let us know what they have decided. I really hope that they will find a way to buy the land, and that Mr. Billson will just go away."

"The Traegons are still searching for any other animals that they think might fit what they are looking for. It would be wonderful if we could find others," Karia shared.

"I think we got lucky finding the little frog, I don't know how many protected animals or plants there could be in one place. I do remember one of the men saying something about some dead trees being a perfect place for an owl. I can't remember what kind he said, but he seemed interested in the area," I said, only half remembering the conversation.

"Well, Dino, we should be getting back. Contact me in the same manner you have when you hear something. I will see if I can find out if any Traegons have seen any owls in Traegonia. We will see you soon."

Karia jumped down from my bed and Juna followed.

"Do you really have to go so soon? Can't you just stay a little while longer?" I asked.

"I am sorry, Dino. I do not want anyone to find us missing. Mim and Sire Argus came to visit and I fear they may check on us. We must be there." Karia answered, as they went to the center of the room and sat together.

Moments later, Karia and Juna were safely back in Traegonia and I was asleep.

Chapter 38
Awaiting the News

Monday morning came and went without any word from the DNR, the Forestry Department, or the Conservation Department. We were all waiting anxiously for any news. It was hard to sit through school wondering if my mother had heard anything yet. Tuesday also came and went without any word. Our hopes were fading with our growing impatience. But on Wednesday afternoon, my mother got a phone call. It was Jake Avers.

"Hi, Jake, how are you?" Anna answered the phone with an excited tone in her voice.

"I'm good. I have some news. I contacted a group called The Illinois Audubon Society. They have a fund that they use specifically to purchase land to be kept for conservation purposes. They want to send someone out to have a look at the land and see if it is something they would like to acquire. They are a non-government organization, but have worked closely with government agencies and other organizations in matters such as this. They would like to see the land tomorrow."

"Tomorrow sounds great. I will go and see Mr. Rhodes today, and make sure it is okay with him. I can call you after that to let you know, and find out a time," Anna responded.

"They have already told me they would like to come around

10:00 a.m. They need to make a decision because there is a board meeting tomorrow night, and they would like to bring it up there. There will also be a town meeting tomorrow night as well. If they don't bring it before the board and town this week, they will have to wait another month," Jake explained. "It would also be good if you and your family could attend both. There are always a few people ready to fight against anything."

"Of course we'll be there. I also have a petition that I had gotten about 150 signatures, opposing the mall development."

"Great! I am betting the developer will attend and try to create opposition.

It is important to have as many in support of saving the land attend also. If you know of any others who are willing to come out, that would be really important," Jake said.

"Of course, I understand completely. I will call everyone I know," Anna responded.

"Call me only if there is a problem. Otherwise, I will see you tomorrow at the Rhodes house. Goodbye."

Anna grabbed her purse and went directly to Mr. Rhodes' house. He was home and seemed to be in a little better mood than he was the other day. He had no problem with the expected visit and in fact, he wanted to be there as well.

"I myself have not walked the property in several years. It will be nice to see what it looks like again." He also agreed to attend the meetings in support of the conservation of the land. "The more I thought about it, I want this land to be here for my grandchildren to see and enjoy, even if we don't live here anymore," Mr. Rhodes told Anna. His change of heart about the land seemed to change his grumpiness and give him a renewed sense of what the future had to offer.

After that visit, Anna went to the forest preserve and told everyone she saw about the meeting. Then she went home to call everyone she knew. If there was one thing Anna was really good at, it was rallying support. She even went to Dino's school and talked to the principal, who agreed to make an announcement to the entire school.

That night, I sat with the crystal and the acorn. I needed to tell Karia what was happening. I fell asleep and when I woke up, I was at the willow with Karia, Juna, Mim, Sire Argus, Oracle Balstar, and the council members. I shared with them the visit that was to take place the next morning, and Mim shared that she knew of a spirit owl family that has lived in Traegonia for as long as she could remember.

"We need these people to see them," I said anxiously.

"Well, I do not know how to get them to go so far from where they nest. They are nearer to where our tree home is," Mim stated.

Antar stood and announced, "I believe I can get Bayalthazar to go to their nesting site and bring back a feather or some other evidence that they exist in these lands."

"That would be great! Maybe he could bring it to where they will be. Maybe they will see it as a sign," I said.

They all looked at each other and smiles spread across their faces. I think we were all excited at what possibilities lay ahead. They thanked me for all of our help, and Karia walked me back to the stone circle. Mim stopped me before I stepped in.

"Dino, make sure your mother receives this." She handed me a smooth rose-colored stone, tied to a bundle of white sage. "Put it somewhere where she will find it. You do not have to let her know you know anything about it. Can you do this?" she whispered.

"Yes, Mim, I can do that." I answered, "But why..." She cut me off placing her finger over my mouth.

"Shh, no questions, please, just do as I ask." She looked over her shoulder. "I will see you soon." Then she walked away.

Karia and I just looked at each other. "You had better go now. We can talk again another time," Karia said, as she and I stepped into the circle and sat down. I woke up in my own bed the next morning.

Chapter 39
A Gift from Her Past

The sun was shining brightly through my window when I woke up. I looked at my clock and noticed I was going to be late for school. I dressed quickly, grabbed my backpack and my jacket, and ran downstairs. No one was in the kitchen. I wondered where my mom was. I put on my jacket, grabbed a granola bar, and shoved it into my pocket. I felt something and pulled it out. It was the stone that Mim had asked me to give to my mom. I looked at it and moved it around in my hand, wondering why Mim would want my mom to have it. I thought it looked like something my mom would have, definitely something she would like. I looked around the kitchen debating on where to leave it. The coffee maker! I knew that she would find it there. I set it down and started for the door. Just as I passed the stairs, my mom startled me.

"Dino, I'm sorry, honey, I overslept! Are you going to be late for school? Do you need a ride?" she asked, sounding rushed.

"No, Mom, I'm just leaving now. I have plenty of time. Do you have any money for lunch?" I asked her.

"Sure, hold on," she ran into the kitchen, came back with a five-dollar bill and handed it to me. "Thanks Mom gotta run. I'll see you after school." She kissed me on the cheek and I left for school.

Anna went back into the kitchen to get ready to leave for her meeting with the man from the Illinois Audubon Society. Mr. Rhodes had agreed to let them come to see the land, and she didn't want to be late. She grabbed a to-go-cup out of the cabinet and began to fill it with coffee. That was when she noticed the gift from Mim. She saw it and looked around as she reached for it. She put it to her nose, closed her eyes, and breathed in deeply. Smelling the fresh white sage, she smiled and looked around the kitchen again, then went to the back door and looked around the backyard, holding the stone and sage to her heart. She whispered, "Thank you, Alistia." She walked back to the coffee pot, filled her cup then she placed the gift into a zipper pocket in her purse, closed it, and headed out the door for her appointment.

Chapter 40
Prophecy Unfolds

Sir Antar went to speak with Bayalthazar. He asked him to retrieve a feather from the nest of the spirit owl. He explained that he would need to bring it to where the people were going to be, and to carefully drop it so that the men would be sure to find it. "If you are able to obtain more than one feather, do so, but if you only have one, you will only have one chance to get it to where they will be able to find it. These are people who want to help us, but I do not think they would understand if they were to see you." Antar spoke seriously to Bayalthazar.

"I am the master of invention. Being unseen is a trait of the Traegons, being invisible is my favorite challenge," he said, as he looked through his optical lens at Antar. This lens made one eye appear much larger than the other, which gave a mischievous look about him. With a crooked grin, he nodded. "It will be done as you ask. Not to worry. When the task is complete, the humans will have been touched by the sacredness of this land."

Antar smiled as well and turned to leave the hidden cave. "You are a good friend and a treasure to Traegonia. Know that we are all grateful for your service to our community." Sir Antar walked out into the sunlight. He took in a deep breath of morning air and looked around at Traegonia from the hilltop. The silence of the forest gave him a true sense of peace and belonging. "There is nothing more beautiful than this land, my home, my world. May we all continue to dwell here in peace and truth." He stepped down the side of the hill and returned to the willow.

Karia, Arbalest, Oracle Balstar, Master Zoal, Mim, Sire Argus, and Juna were all standing in the willow's garden, discussing the plan when Sir Antar entered. "My visit went well. Bayalthazar assured me the task is as good as completed."

"Excellent," responded Oracle Balstar.

"I know that Dino will not be at the meeting, but I still feel we should be there to see that it all goes as it should," Karia stated.

"I think that would be acceptable. Maybe Sire Argus would like to accompany Arbalest on this travel," Oracle Balstar suggested.

"I would like to go as well," Mim strongly requested. Everyone looked in her direction, including Karia.

Karia tilted her head. "Mim? You really wish to come?"

"Yes, Karia, do you think I am not strong enough to handle this task?" Mim asked Karia. She smiled and the tone in Mim's voice deterred any others from trying to tell her otherwise.

Karia always felt her Mim was the strongest she-Traegon she had ever known, and realized it was a poor question to ask. "No, Mim, actually I would be honored to accompany you on this task." Karia smiled at Mim.

Mim smiled back and the four of them headed off to prepare a wagon. Juna stood silently and glanced from the ground to Oracle Balstar. Balstar was looking directly at Juna.

"Don't just stand there! You will be left behind," Oracle told Juna. "Team, you have one more. He will be an excellent hunter one day himself. Zoal, summon my dragonfly to accompany them. He will be able to go where they cannot and will not raise suspicion." Before long, the team was on their way to monitor the meeting.

Chapter 41
The Confirmation

Anna was the first to arrive at Mr. Rhodes' home. She knocked at his door and a few minutes later, he answered.

"Good morning, Anna. It's a beautiful day, wouldn't you say?"

"It sure is," Anna replied, a bit surprised at his unusually happy demeanor.

"You're a little early. Come on in and have a cup of coffee," Mr. Rhodes invited her.

"Well, thank you, I would like that very much," Anna answered. She stepped into the house. She had never been inside before and was excited to see it. The house was an old farmhouse with beautiful wide wood trim, and old world charm.

"This is a sweet home you have, Mr. Rhodes."

"Thank you, but I cannot take credit for the decorating. My wife took care of all that. She always said a home was an extension of a woman's heart." From the tone of his voice, he was clearly thinking of his wife.

"Well then, she must have had a beautiful heart," Anna said, taking a sip of her coffee.

"That she did." Mr. Rhodes smiled. They sat and talked and drank coffee until there was a knock at the door. It was Jake Avers and another man, who Jake introduced as Tom Merl. Tom was with the Illinois Audubon Society, and was very excited to see the land and what it had to offer. Tom shook hands with Mr. Rhodes and Anna.

"It's really nice to meet you. I looked up the property and drove the perimeter earlier this week after I spoke with Jake. We are very interested in acquiring this land for preservation purposes. I just need to walk the property to see what wildlife and plant life might exist here. So if we're all ready, let's get going."

They all walked out the front door together and walked around to the back of the house. Jake and Tom walked along the edge of the forest and peered into the woods. "You said the river runs through the property. Can you take me there?" Tom requested.

"Of course," answered Jake. "Follow me." Jake led as if he knew the property completely.

Anna and Mr. Rhodes followed behind. They walked into the forest behind the house, walking slowly and deliberately, looking carefully through the trees, at the ground, at the plants, and all around. They walked for a long while and finally reached the river. They already knew that the Blanchard Cricket Frog lived in the area, of this they had proof. As they made their way back through the forest, they heard something in the trees above them. They all stopped and listened, looking up through the dense trees. They didn't hear anything else, but stayed still for a while longer. Out of the air floated a single white feather. All four of them watched the feather gently float down, but not one of them had seen where it came from. When it was within reach, Jake walked toward it and grabbed it out of the air. He walked back and handed it to Tom. Tom looked closely at it, he knew as soon as he saw it what type of bird it was from. Tom closed his hand around the feather and looked at the others.

"What is it?" Anna asked.

"It is a feather from a Common Barn Owl, which is not so common anymore. The population of these owls has been steadily decreasing in this area, due to the development in the areas they would normally occupy."

Tom looked around. He pointed to a cluster of dead trees that could be seen poking out across the river. "See those dead trees over there? That is exactly the type of habitat that would serve as a perfect nesting site. I have no doubt that there are Common Barn Owls in this area, and I think this is proof enough." Even Mr. Rhodes seemed impressed by the findings.

The group continued to walk back to the house. The silence and solitude were incredibly peaceful, and each one of them seemed touched by the beauty that surrounded them. Not far from the river, Anna noticed a large dragonfly fluttering through the trees. Her mind began to wander back to a time long ago, when she was a child. She always believed in miracles, Santa, fairies, and the creatures she had told Dino about. Even as she grew, she held on to her beliefs. They comforted her, and so did the dragonfly on that afternoon. It flew in and out of the trees and came close to her several times, as they continued to walk.

"Anna, stop!" Mr. Rhodes called from behind her.

"What is it, Mr. Rhodes?" Anna asked, turning around. The others heard what was going on and stopped as well.

"There is a big dragonfly on your head," he continued. She reached up to touch her head.

"Wait, Anna, don't!" Tom called. He slowly approached her. "Just stand still. I want to take a closer look before it flies away." As he came closer, his eyes widened. "Alright, this is the final confirmation for me," he stated.

"What is?" asked Mr. Rhodes.

Dino C. Crisanti

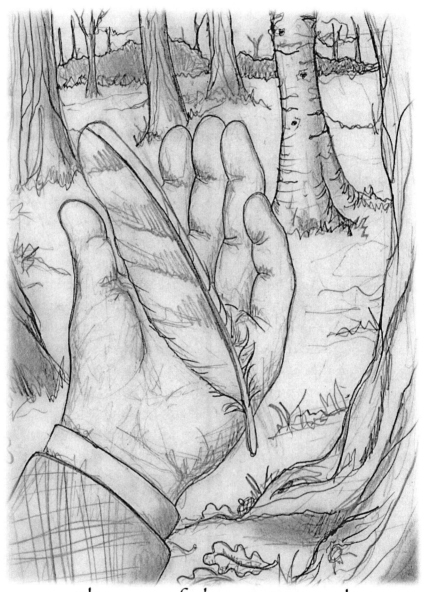

Glimpse of the Spirit Owl

"This is a Hines Emerald Dragonfly. This is a federally protected species, and there are several organizations researching and
actively protecting them. This dragonfly is an excellent indicator
species of a quality habitat. Mr. Rhodes, I am going to be completely honest with you. This land is perfect for the preservation
of so many species. In just a short time, we know of at least three
species that are listed as, at the least, protected. This land is clearly
critical to life. We would absolutely like to purchase this land from
you, and we can guarantee that if you were to come back here in
five, ten, even twenty years from now, this land will always remain
as it is today. As soon as I get back to my office, I will have our
attorney draw up an offer to purchase. I hope you will seriously
consider allowing us to buy and protect this land."

Tom looked at Mr. Rhodes, hoping for some indication of
what his answer might be. Mr. Rhodes smiled and the dragonfly
lifted off from Anna's head, landed on Mr. Rhodes' hand, then flew
away.

The group returned to the house. "Well, I guess this is it. Thank
you, Mr. Rhodes, for your time and for the care you have given this
land over the last thirty-six years. I hope to see you at the meeting
tonight," Tom said, reaching out his hand.

Mr. Rhodes shook Tom's hand and told him, "I'll be there, Mr.
Merl. You can count on it."

"We will also be there. See you tonight," said Anna. They all
went their separate ways.

We left our house at 6:00 that evening. There were two meetings we were to attend and we arrived early to meet Mr. Rhodes,
Jake Avers, and Tom Merl. We all felt very positive about how the
evening would go. We watched as many others entered the building
and took their seats. Many of them smiled and waved at my mom,
as she had invited a lot of them to attend and show their support.

Then the door opened and in walked Mr. Billson, and several other men who came with him. He glared at my mother and me.

"Why is he here?" I asked my mother.

Mr. Merl answered, "There was a public notice about the meeting tonight. He must have seen it. I am sure he is going to try and stop the land acquisition." Mr. Billson walked up to Mr. Rhodes. He spoke to him for a few moments and handed him a letter-sized envelope. Mr. Rhodes took the letter and walked back to his seat. He opened it and looked at the papers. It was a letter stating that Billson Developers would consider giving him a little more money, but he wanted to see the offer from the Audubon Society first.

We went to our seats as the city council members entered the room and took their seats at the long table in the front of the room. The Board President selected the Secretary to read the notes from the last meeting, and what was on the agenda for tonight. It was pretty boring and I started to get restless. My mom kept nudging me, telling me to sit still. I continued to look around the room, and finally noticed Quinn sitting in the back with his mom and dad. I so wanted to be sitting with him right about now. Finally, I caught his attention and we started mouthing words to each other, stuff about school and making faces, just to pass the time.

Then I heard a voice say, "And for our final matter of the evening."

It caught my attention and I turned around. "The board would like to bring before our residents the matter of the Rhodes' property on the outside of town. This is more of an informational formality and to open the floor for discussion, the matter of the Illinois Audubon Society purchasing the thirty acres of land on the edge of town, owned for the last thirty-six years by Mr. and Mrs. Rhodes. Mr. Rhodes was approached by Billson Developers, who wish to purchase the land to build a Super Mall, whereby clearing and leveling all of the land.

"The Illinois Audubon Society feels the land would be better left to serve the local wildlife. It is our understanding that a certain species of frog was found on the land that was all but extinct, and is now beginning to grow in numbers. It is also our understanding that there may very well be other species, plant and animal, that may also inhabit these thirty acres. Mr. Rhodes has indicated to us that his decision as to who he will be selling the property to will be The Illinois Audubon Society Land Trust. The land will remain in its current state, and remain protected for all to enjoy." He continued, "As a village government, we do not typically get involved in land sales, but due to the size of the parcel and its possible impact to the community, we felt we should inform the community. Now, does anyone have any comments or questions regarding this issue?"

"I object!" a familiar voice came from the far side of the room. It was Mr. Billson, and he didn't look happy. "My proposition for the building of this Super Mall would have more of a benefit for this town and the community than leaving it to some critters that most of us will never even see. This project will bring more tax revenue into this town than it has ever seen. It will bring people from all over the country to spend their money here. This mall is proposed to be one of the biggest in the country, with an indoor amusement park and over 400 stores. You won't have to travel to do your shopping anymore. Everything will be right in your backyard. There will be more restaurants in one place than there are in this whole town and more jobs available to the people who live here. Who wouldn't want this for their town?"

Mr. Billson looked around the room. There was a low growl of voices in discussion. I looked around too. *Are they even considering this?* I wondered to myself.

Finally, my mom stood up. I saw Mr. Billson give her a nasty look. "Mr. Billson and members of the community, I have lived here all my life, and one of the very things that has made me love this town is the quiet country feel, the land that wraps our town in beauty each season; the plants and animals that we see, and those we may never see. This is what I love about our town, our home. Since I was a child, I have been going to this forest preserve bordered by Mr. Rhodes' land. I have spent hours and days just enjoying the beauty and peacefulness. And now as an adult and mother, I have the opportunity to show this to my own child. Having this so-called Super Mall would take all of this away and replace it with a lot of noise and light pollution, more cars and traffic.

"I don't really mind that people from all over the country don't come and visit. I love my quiet peaceful community and wish for it to remain this way. From my perspective, I don't see any real benefits to the people of this community. I do understand that if you are looking through eyes with dollar signs blocking your view, then this might look like a good idea. But there are a lot of strip malls and storefronts that are already standing empty. How do you think it would look to have a giant vacant mall as the first thing you see when you come into our town? What are you going to do with it then? People will always come to a park or a preserve. It doesn't cost anything. It's an escape from the craziness of daily life, and it's a tool to teach and learn. I ask each of you, look into your heart and tell me, when you are driving down the road in the fall, which would you prefer to see?, the beautiful trees with their brilliant colors or a shopping mall in the middle of a giant parking lot."

My mom took a breath. A small clap came from the back of the room. There was Quinn, who always liked my mom and her cookies. Quinn's mother looked at him, stood, and began to clap also. Then Quinn's dad, Mom's friends, Pat and Ron from the DNR, Charlie, everyone, they all wanted the forest to stay, and one by one, they each took a stand for their community and for nature. They became the voices for the creatures who couldn't speak for themselves. For the Blanchard Cricket Frogs, for the fish in the river, for all the animals without voices we can hear. I felt a tingle through my body. There wouldn't need to be a fight, because at least the people from our little town believed in the importance of this place, and really that was what mattered, because we live here. Mr. Billson looked around the room with a mean look on his face as he glared at my mother and me. I stuck my tongue out, which my mom always hated. But she didn't see me and I didn't think she would have been that mad anyway. Mr. Billson grabbed his jacket and papers and motioned for his people to leave.

"Let's get out of here and leave these lousy tree-huggers to them-selves," a woman overheard him say.

"Hugging a tree has more power in it than hugging a concrete wall, Mr. Billson," the woman pointed out.

Billson turned and walked away. He was so angry, he pushed open the door and it slammed right back into the men behind him. When he walked past a row of bushes, he heard a low deep whisper. He couldn't make it out and thought it was one of the men who were with him, but when he stopped and turned around, he saw the men were still far behind him. He turned to continue when he heard it again, and this time it was perfectly clear. "Get out of this town. You are not welcome here, by its people, and you are absolutely not welcome by its wildlife."

Billson looked around, startled. Suddenly, two large black ravens flew out of the bushes and startled him. He ran off to his car with Sable and the raven who would one day become Karia's not far be-hind. Billson fumbled for his keys and quickly got into his car, and the two birds flew off into the night.

Mr. Merl approached my mother and father, who were talking to some of their friends and the people from the council board.

"One down. We just have our board meeting next, which should be a piece of cake compared to this one. We already know we are interested in buying the land."

"Where is this meeting being held?" my dad asked.

"The DNR office has graciously offered us the use of their office. The meeting won't take long, but since our offices are so far away, we will be attending via phone. We have about a half hour before the meeting is set to begin. I am going to head over and get set up," Mr. Merl said.

"I'll follow you over if you don't mind," stated Mr. Rhodes.

"That would be just fine." The two men left the building. People were happy and spoke with a sense of victory in their voices. Me, I was relieved. It was over and Traegonia would be safe for a long time to come.

There was just one glitch that came up at the meeting with the people from the Illinois Audubon Society. They definitely wanted the thirty-six acres and were willing to give Mr. Rhodes a bit more than what Billson Developers had offered, but they didn't want the house. Mr. Rhodes' face dropped when he heard that. "Well, Mr. Rhodes, you can still sell the house and make some extra money on that," the voice offered over the phone.

"Well sure," said Mr. Rhodes. My mom looked at Mr. Rhodes and knew what he must be feeling. She knew how much the house meant to him, and how much he was looking forward to moving on, and moving in with his daughter. My mom looked at my dad with a pleading look. He hadn't even seen her at first, but when he did, he knew immediately what she was thinking. The next day, there was a For Sale sign in our front yard.

Chapter 42
Final Chapter

Our house sold relatively quickly, and we were able to move a few weeks after school was out. I loved the house, and I especially loved being close to the woods every day. I remember waking up very early one morning, to the birds chirping and the sound of the warm breeze blowing the blinds on my window. I looked out my bedroom window and saw my mother kneeling down at the edge of the yard near the woods. I watched her for a while, and I could swear I saw something small moving in front of her, but my view was blocked by her body. I went downstairs and stood quietly on the back porch. I could hear her talking, and I thought I heard others talking too, but it was too muffled. I wondered who she was talking to, but no matter how hard I listened, I couldn't make out the voices, or what they were saying. I always knew that she loved the forest. She always taught me to respect the Earth and all of the creatures who lived there, and I know she was glad we lived here now. I saw her raise her hand, hold it straight out, and then bring it to her heart. My eyes opened wide and I gasped. She knew of them, and she probably knew long before I did. Was Mim her friend, or one of the Madam's? We never talked about it, but I believe she just might have been the first one.

From that day on, I saw Karia and Juna a few times a week.

I still took my adventures in the woods, and we would spend our time talking and playing. They would watch me draw in my journal. We became the best of friends; a friendship I could share only with them. I taught them about our world and they taught me about theirs. I never shared them with anyone, until now. Whether you see them or not, they are there. Not just the Traegons, but species of so many different kinds. They deserve to live and we must be their voices. I knew that I wanted to grow up to be a part of the effort to ensure that all creatures, both known and unknown, those living and those who used to live would always have a place on this Earth. Hopefully, there would always be land unaffected by our human existence, where they could thrive and survive. It is my mission to teach and to help others understand the importance of protecting our Earth. I have never forgotten what Karia, Juna, and the Traegons taught me, and I will continue to share their story with all who dare to believe.

If you would like more information about conservation contact:

The Illinois Audubon Society
P.O. Box 2547
Springfield, IL 62708
217-544-BIRD

The Mission of the Audubon Society is to promote the perpetuation and appreciation of native plants and animals and habitats that support them.

CPSIA information can be obtained at www.ICGtesting.com
Printed in the USA
LVOW07s1151300913

354622LV00002B/3/P